Encore Murder

MARIAN BABSON

Encore Murder

A THOMAS·DUNNE BOOK

St. Martin's Press
New York

Library of Congress Cataloging-in-Publication Data

Babson, Marian.
    Encore murder / by Marian Babson.
       p.   cm.
    "A Thomas Dunne book."
    ISBN 0-312-04964-1
    I. Title.
    PS3552.A25E5   1990
    813'.54—dc20   90-37332
                                                  CIP

First published in Great Britain by William Collins Sons & Co. Limited

First U.S. Edition: October 1990
10 9 8 7 6 5 4 3 2 1

For Beatrice Monteleone, Shirley Hecht, and all those other friends (I think) who threatened me with dire penalties if Trixie and Evangeline didn't take an encore.

CHAPTER 1

'Griselda von Kirstenberg,' Evangeline said severely, 'has had her face lifted so many times that the last time she visited Chinatown, three people asked her for directions—in Cantonese.'

I sighed. I had known it wasn't going to be easy. And she hadn't even heard the bad news yet.

'Evangeline, listen to me—' Nevertheless, I persisted. Someone had to break it to her—and everyone else was chicken.

'Evangeline, the moment of truth is approaching. If you know what the truth is.'

'The truth?' She gave the word the 'ha-and-ba-ag?' treatment. 'Trixie, are you implying that my veracity has ever been in doubt?'

'Only among those who really know you.'

Evangeline sniffed and ostentatiously returned to studying her script.

The telephone rang. I picked up the receiver absently. We all make these mistakes. 'Hello?'

'Mother, what do you think about écru taffeta?'

'It sounds lovely, dear.' We had already been through this with lavender chiffon, rose wild silk, leaf-green organza and silver satin. It would take more than écru taffeta to stampede me now.

'That's what I think. I'll be around with the swatch and sketches just as soon as I have a minute, but Hugh—'

There was a slight commotion in the background.

'Yes, darling, I'm coming. Sorry, Mother, I must fly or we'll be late for a meeting with the angels. At least, we hope they're going to be angels. Yes, darling, I'm coming. Goodbye, Mother.'

Evangeline had lowered her script and was watching me. Her curiosity got the better of her. 'What is it this time?'

'Ecru taffeta.'

'That would be a mistake. It's not her colour.'

'For me, not her. I've told you, she's wearing white.'

Evangeline snorted. 'If she's really entitled to a white wedding at her age, I shouldn't think she'd want to advertise the fact.'

There are some remarks it's best to ignore—especially when you know they've been intended to start a fight. Or perhaps to change the subject.

'We were talking about Griselda von Kirstenberg,' I said firmly.

'Or Grisly, as so many of her friends preferred to call her.'

'Evangeline—'

'Oh, very well. I can see I'll have no peace until you've had your say. Go ahead, I'll play straight man: Tell me, Trixie, what is that tedious bore up to now?'

'She's writing her memoirs.'

'Is she?' Evangeline's eyes narrowed dangerously. 'I hadn't realized that science had perfected asbestos paper.'

'Furthermore, she's on her way over here.'

'Here?' She's coming to London?' Evangeline shook her head. 'Who says witches can't cross water? The Jet Age has a lot to answer for.'

The telephone rang again.

'Mother, I nearly forgot. The invitations—'

'I posted them this morning. As soon as the RSVPs start arriving, we'll be able to give the caterers an idea of the numbers.'

'Oh, thank heavens! I don't know how I could have forgotten. But I left in such a hurry this morning . . . Yes, darling, I'm coming . . .' The line went dead.

'Oh, for God's sake, tell her to elope!' Evangeline snapped.

'She's rung off,' I said, quite proud of myself for producing such an English phrase.

'She'll be back,' Evangeline said darkly. 'I don't know how she does it. All over London you hear people complaining about the telephone service: calls cut off, telephones ringing when no one at the receiving end can hear them, false busy signals, crossed lines—and yet Martha always manages to get through.'

'She was always resourceful,' I said proudly, 'even as a child.'

Evangeline snorted. Again ostentatiously, she returned to the script in her hand. I recognized that it was not the script that she was supposed to be studying, but refused to let that throw me. After all, there was no rush about the revival of *Arsenic and Old Lace*; we hadn't acquired a theatre yet. Quite frankly, I suspected that Hugh had muddled his priorities and was placing the production below the wedding.

Late love had hit our producer and our daughter hard. Despite, or perhaps because of, the fact that neither was in their first youth.

I supposed one had to make allowances for them, but I was not prepared to indulge Evangeline, too.

'You don't give Martha enough credit,' I challenged her. 'Just think, she might be writing *her* autobiography, instead of merely getting married. Plenty of stars' children are doing that now. And then where would we be?'

'Precisely where we are now,' Evangeline said coldly. 'I would, as usual, be trying to concentrate on my work and you would, as usual, be bitching at me about something over which I have—and never have had—any control.' She shook the script at me and then turned a page and became utterly absorbed again. Too absorbed.

'OK,' I said, 'I give up. What *are* you playing with there?'

'I am studying my script.'

'What script?'

The telephone rang again and I seriously considered not answering it, but it kept on ringing.

'Go ahead,' Evangeline jeered. 'It might be of world-shaking importance. She may have decided to change the colour of the bows on the bouquets.'

'Hello?' There was always the possibility that it might be someone else.

'With lavender satin piping, Mother. Ecru taffeta with lavender satin piping. And stiff net underskirts.'

'Yes, dear.' I closed my eyes, trying *not* to visualize it.

'Gretna Green . . .' Evangeline muttered like an incantation. 'Las Vegas . . . Anywhere but here!'

The dialling tone was buzzing in my ear again. I stayed there with my eyes closed and the receiver buzzing at me. It was the most peaceful moment I had had all day.

'It's no use your standing there pretending you're still listening to Martha's ravings,' Evangeline said. 'I can tell she's gone—your colour has come back.'

'Come back . . .' I echoed faintly. Something stirred at the back of my mind. 'That's what else I wanted to tell you about Griselda von Kirstenberg—she's planning a comeback.'

'Grisly is always planning a comeback. She has spent the past forty years quaintly imagining that she has something to come back *to*.'

'Oh, come on, she hasn't been out of work *that* long. She was on that television soap opera up until about ten years ago.'

'Daytime TV!' Evangeline curled her lip, displaying the

eyeteeth she would cheerfully have sacrificed to have won that part herself.

There was a sudden crash from overhead and then a rhythmic thumping that threatened to crack the ceiling.

'You had to teach them to tap dance,' Evangeline said bitterly.

'How was I to know we were going to stay here for the rest of the winter?' Our original plans had only been for a two-week holiday, but events had steam-rollered us into a completely new mode of life. I was already beginning to suspect that we would never leave England again. And I didn't care. All things considered, the living was easy.

'Just how is it,' Evangeline asked suspiciously, 'that you are suddenly such an expert on the doings of Griselda von Kirstenberg? I didn't know you were such good friends.'

'Neither did I,' I admitted. 'But she rang me last night and I began to think I must be her long-lost cousin.'

'Ah yes, of course!' Evangeline's face cleared. 'It's all so sudden that we haven't had a chance to get used to it yet, but you're going to have to watch your step from now on.'

'What do you mean?' She'd lost me.

'You are about to discover,' she prophesied darkly, 'that you have more friends than you ever dreamt. Now that you're going to be the mother-in-law of one of the most successful theatrical producers in London.'

'Good heavens!' I'd never thought of that. 'I do believe you could be right.' It would certainly explain Griselda's unaccustomed warmth.

'Of course I'm right.' Evangeline rustled her script irritably. 'And I'll tell you something else: Martha is about to find that *she* has more friends than she ever dreamt of—and she's so naïve she'll actually believe they *are* her friends. She won't be able to cope at all.'

'She'll learn.' Especially with me keeping guard over her. Another reason why I couldn't leave England and abandon her to her fate. Not that I wanted to, in any case. Life had suddenly developed more possibilities than any time I had known since some half-mad studio executive who thought he was in love with me had begun a campaign to win me an Oscar—for Best Dramatic Actress.

'The hard way, I'm afraid.' Evangeline sounded quite gleeful about the prospect. Life had opened up again for her, too.

'You're the expert on that.'

'Dear Trixie.' Evangeline flapped the script ostentatiously again. 'You always have an answer to everything.'

'All right.' I gave up. 'What have you got there?'

Before she could answer, the bell rang. I was so conditioned by this time that I picked up the phone automatically and it took the dialling tone to make me realize that it was the doorbell I had heard.

'That must be her now.' I went to answer it.

'Who?' Evangeline spoke in her most deadly Ethel Barrymore tones, as though the mere sound of her disapproval could stop events in their tracks—possibly even reverse them.

'Griselda von Kirstenberg.' At least, she had halted me. 'I told you she was coming over here.'

'I didn't know you meant here, *here*. I thought you meant here, London. And that was bad enough.'

'You weren't listening properly,' I weaseled. Maybe I could have explained more clearly, but it had suddenly seemed the better part of valour to present Evangeline with a *fait accompli*.

The bell pealed imperiously and I started again for the door.

'Stay right where you are!' Evangeline thundered. 'I will not have that woman in my house!'

'It's Jasper's house,' I pointed out. 'And we can't leave her standing on the doorstep. She'll make a scene. You know

Jasper wants to keep on good terms with his neighbours—
and we've had enough scenes around here.'

As Evangeline still glowered, I turned on my heel. This
time I made it to the front door and opened it—not cautiously enough.

'Treexie, dollink!' I was almost smothered in a whirlwind
of sable reeking of something extravagantly expensive with
a musk base. I was so busy choking that she succeeded in
kissing me on both cheeks and was trying for an encore
before I managed to twist free. We definitely were not on
those terms. In fact, the first few times I had met her, she
had refused to acknowledge the introduction on the grounds
that I was an escaped tassel-twirler from Minsky's who
had no business trying to mix with her betters. Me, an
established Broadway musical comedy star, who'd never
been near Minsky's in her life—far less twirled a tassel.

'Und how is my beloffed Evangeline?'

'Waiting for you with open arms,' I said.

'So?' Not even *her* ego would let her swallow that one.
She'd made a few devastating remarks about Evangeline,
too, in her time. But, let's face it, we only remember our
own bad reviews.

'Go right in,' I said, keeping a nice safe distance behind,
but not so far back that I couldn't watch the fur fly.

Even so, I cringed when she gave it the corny old theatrical
entrance: a dead pause in the doorway, one hand high on
the frame, the other hand grasping the opposite frame just
below hip level. It gave the audience time to focus on you
and maximized the impact of your entrance—but it also
made you the perfect target.

Evangeline, however, seemed to be on her best behaviour.
At least, nothing flew through the air, despite the temptation. Not yet.

'EE-van-gee-line, dollink!' Griselda broke the pose and
moved forward, both hands outstretched.

'Griselda.' Evangeline had taken the precaution of moving behind the armchair in the corner. To embrace her— or reach her at all—Griselda would have had to take a flying leap over the back of the chair. 'How . . . surprising . . . to see you here.'

'Surrprrizing?' Recognizing defeat, Griselda let her arms drop. 'But I am just arrived in town. Naturally, I must see my dearest friends.'

'Oh?' Evangeline turned slowly and surveyed the room, as though looking for them.

'Do sit down, Griselda.' I tried to cling to the amenities. 'Would you like some tea?'

'What a pity we've just finished ours,' Evangeline said. 'It will be quite cold now. And we've given the maid the afternoon off.'

'No! No!' Even Griselda could recognize a hint when bludgeoned over the head with it. 'I have just had lunch. Nothing more is necessary.'

'Well, sit down, anyway,' I said.

'Oh?' Evangeline raised an eyebrow. 'Must you stay?'

'Ah-ha-ha—' Griselda sank down on the sofa, shrugging off her sable coat and stripping off her black elbow-length gloves with an expertise that would have been envied at Minsky's. 'So droll, Evangeline. As always.'

I thought of offering her a drink, but Evangeline caught the thought and sent me a look hard enough to knock out a couple of teeth. I closed my mouth, leaving the words unspoken.

An ominous silence lengthened until I was delighted to hear the telephone ring. I snatched it up and instinctively turned my back to the others. 'Hello—'

'Mother, listen—I've got something to tell you.' Martha's voice was high-pitched and shaking. She sounded on the verge of tears.

'Darling, what's the matter?'

'She's changed her mind again,' Evangeline said wearily. 'We can only hope she'll run out of colours soon.'

'Darling—?' I waved my hand behind my back to hush Evangeline. At the other end of the line, I could hear deep breaths that were threatening to turn into sobs. 'What is it you want to tell me?'

'I can't!' Martha wailed. 'I can't! It's too awful! I'm coming home! Mother, I'm coming home!' She broke the connection.

Nothing could be that bad, I tried to reassure myself as I replaced the receiver and turned around.

'Ach, yes, the child.' Griselda's speculative gaze slid from me to Evangeline. 'What a chapter that will make.'

'I have no intention of mentioning her,' Evangeline said coldly.

'Ach, no, dollink,' Griselda purred. 'Not in your book. In mine.'

CHAPTER 2

If looks could kill, there was no doubt about it, Griselda von Kirstenberg would be lying stretched out on the carpet and once more Evangeline and I would be wondering what to do with a dead body.

Fortunately—or unfortunately, as the case may be—our combined glares had no such effect. Griselda just sat there giving cats a bad name by the purry little sounds of satisfaction coming from her throat.

'One of the great secrets of the cinema world—' Griselda kept rubbing it in. 'Unsuspected . . . unpublished . . . until now.'

'I will kill you,' Evangeline said. 'Slowly.'

'You'll have to get in line,' I said grimly. 'I'm going to kill her first.'

'Such fire! Such passion!' Griselda mocked. 'After all these years. What does it matter now?'

'It matters to Martha,' I said. 'She's just getting married, starting a new life in a different country—'

'It matters to me, too,' Evangeline said. 'For myself, never mind Martha. I haven't guarded my reputation all these years to see it flung to the four winds now.'

'I see we understand each other.' It was the same line and the same nasty smile Griselda had used as the evil Baroness in *Swastikas over Freedom*. Suddenly, I hated her as much now as Middle America had hated her then. She had managed to salvage her reputation by dying repentant in every film and giving her life to save the hero, sometimes for Love and sometimes because she had Seen the Light. It had been a close-run race, but worth the risk: there had been big money available in the 'forties for those who had been willing to appear as Nazi villains and villainesses. It had never occurred to me before that it had been absolute type-casting for Griselda—except for the bit about repentance at the end.

'Ach, how well I remember those happy days on the set of *Let Love Linger!* I was working on the set next door, on *Do You Remember?* and we shared the same wardrobe girl. Ach, all those whispered conversations you had with her in dark corners—and every day she was letting out the waist seams in your costumes.'

'I have a headache,' Evangeline said distantly. 'I must go and lie down.'

'Ach, ja! You did so much of that, too. We were always laughing—it was so appropriate, the title of your picture. Your love episode was indeed lingering . . .'

Evangeline shot her another killing look, but it bounced right off the invisible armour.

'Und poor Trixie—' She turned her poisonous attention to me. 'So unsuspecting, so trusting. Such fantastic dancing —all that energy. But always flinging herself around like that. No child could ever keep a grasp in *her* womb . . .'

'You were right,' I told Evangeline. 'It was a mistake to let her in.'

'We must fumigate the house,' Evangeline said. 'As soon as she has left. Which I trust will be immediately.'

'Your Director on that film was Trixie's husband.' Griselda had no intention of leaving, she was enjoying herself too much. 'Your best friend's husband—it was almost a family affair.'

'I'm going to count to three,' Evangeline said. 'If you aren't out that door by then, I will not be responsible for the consequences.'

'Ach, but we have so much to talk about . . .' She smiled at us unpleasantly. 'We have not yet begun to scratch the surface.'

'There'll be more than the surface scratched—' I backed Evangeline—'if you don't get out of here.'

'Shall I portray it as a callous star who did not want her own child?' Griselda wondered aloud. 'Or is it heartwarming, touching? The first surrogate mother.'

'Three!' Evangeline said. 'Let's get her, Trixie!'

'What happened to one and two?' Griselda was startled.

'Who cares?' Evangeline started forward. 'Come on, Trixie. No jury on earth would convict us!'

'So droll!' Griselda laughed nervously, watching Evangeline pick up the poker from the fireplace. 'But perhaps you should listen to what else I have to say.'

'There's more?' I couldn't believe the woman's nerve.

'We must be practical.' She spoke directly to Evangeline. 'We have much to discuss.'

'Oh no we haven't,' Evangeline said. 'Out!'

'But consider. You are writing your memoirs. I am writing

mine. We lived through the same era. Sometimes we worked on the same films. We have so much in common ... memories in common.'

'Are you suggesting—?' Evangeline drew herself up majestically, brandishing the poker like a sceptre, although she was still holding it like a club. 'Are you daring to suggest that we—we divide up our memories? Or do you want us to pool them?' Either suggestion, her tone implied, was unthinkable.

'Ach, no.' Griselda shrugged a still-elegant shoulder. 'I have no need of your recollections. I have always kept a diary. It is all there.'

'You would have,' Evangeline said. 'As dear Mae West advised, "Keep a diary and some day it will keep you." You were just the sort to take that advice to heart.'

'She wasn't the only one,' I said in disgust. 'The bookstores are full of it these days. All our colleagues are publishing their kiss-at-sixteen-and-tell-at-seventy memoirs.'

The icy silence suddenly made me realize what I had just said.

'I didn't mean you, of course, Evangeline,' I said hastily.

'Nor me, of course,' Griselda purred. 'Present company is always excepted.'

'In your case, I could make an exception of the exception,' I said. Why did she have to come here stirring up all this trouble?

'We do not have to concern ourselves with Trixie's opinions.' Griselda spoke over my head to Evangeline. Her little sneer relegated me to the ranks of those who scrawled their names with difficulty, moved their lips when they read and had to take their shoes off if the count went above ten. So much for Trixie. 'It would be better if we were to speak in private.'

'Trixie lives here,' Evangeline said. 'I have no secrets from her.'

'Not any more, ja?' Griselda's sneer was turned on Evangeline now. 'How sweet that you have achieved such rapport . . . in your declining years.'

'Out!' Evangeline brandished the poker. 'Out, this very minute!'

'Perhaps I shall leave now.' Languidly, Griselda drew on her furs. 'You will require time to consider the situation.' She stood up and sauntered to the door. 'Then you will see that I am right.'

'Out!' The poker whizzed past Griselda's head, so close that I winced.

'You do not frighten me. I leave only because there are other old friends that I must call upon. I go now to have tea with Beauregard Sylvester. I have not seen him since we made *Sunset on the Somme* just before he moved to this country.'

'Out!'

'I go—' Griselda paused in the doorway and whirled about, doing her semi-spreadeagle pose again. 'But I will return. Und, next time, you will listen to me.'

She knew a good exit line when she uttered one. She whirled again and was gone. The front door slammed.

'Brandy!' Evangeline gasped, dropping the poker and sinking into an armchair.

I rushed to pour her a glass and poured one for myself as well. It had been quite a scene.

'Anyway,' I said, 'she's kept her figure. You've got to hand her that.' Of course, she wouldn't have gone around posing in doorways like that if she hadn't.

'Kept her figure and kept her diary.' Evangeline sipped thoughtfully at her drink. 'Grisly always was up to something. I know her technique of old. This was just a softening up visit. I wonder what she really wants.'

'I seem to remember that she's announced that she was writing her memoirs before.' I had been doing some thinking. 'Several times before.' But she never seems to get very far with the project. Maybe she thinks she'd be able to finish it if she had someone else working on it with her. Maybe she's going to suggest that you collaborate on a joint memoir.'

'Never!'

'Well, it was just an idea.' For a moment, I'd thought Evangeline was going to pick up the poker again and use it on me.

'You're right about one thing, though. Grisly announces she's writing those memoirs about every five years. There's the usual flurry of publicity and then nothing is ever heard about it again—until the next announcement. You know what that means, don't you?'

'Pay-offs?' I guessed it right away and wondered why I'd never thought of it before. Probably because I hadn't been interested enough. 'Hush money!'

'Don't be so mealy-mouthed, Trixie. Blackmail! She's been systematically working her way through her old associates collecting money for *not* publishing her diaries.'

'Well, if she's worked her way down to us, she must be scraping the bottom of the barrel.'

'And Beauregard—' Evangeline snorted with sudden laughter. 'She'll have her work cut out trying to get any money out of *him*.'

'Poor Griselda.' I couldn't help laughing, too. 'I'd like to be a fly on the wall for *that* meeting.'

'She'll probably wind up paying for the drinks herself.' Evangeline was restored to good humour. 'Grisly must have forgotten what he's like. It's just as well she kept diaries— she's slipping.'

'She certainly is if she thinks we're going to pay her anything. After all, it might not be so terrible if the story came out. Martha has always suspected the truth and now she knows—and she was the important one. We can call Grisly's bluff. Tell her to publish and be damned.'

There was the most wonderful feeling of lightness and relief as I said that, realizing that the burden of fear of discovery I had carried all these years had been lifted at last. Martha had finally admitted that she knew and that it didn't matter. I was her mother, despite the fact that Evangeline had borne her. None of us were yet completely comfortable now that the veil of secrecy was gone, but we would learn to live with it.

And it had happened just in time, now that Griselda was upon us with her nasty blackmailing ways. Despite Evangeline's fears, it would take more than an ancient scandal to destroy her reputation. And it wasn't as though Martha had followed us into the profession—no one would even be very interested. Her husband-to-be had guessed the truth almost immediately upon meeting us and it hadn't made any difference to him. With Hugh by her side, Martha should be able to face the public disclosure.

'It will never come to that,' Evangeline said. 'She'd never go to all the work of writing a book just to spite us because we won't pay. There are still enough around who will, and she must be resigned to the occasional failure.'

'You're right.' I was greatly cheered. 'She's only bluffing. We'll call her bluff and she won't be able to do a thing about it.'

'We have nothing to worry about,' Evangeline confirmed. 'Of course –' she grinned evilly—'I'm not so sure about Beau.'

'I'll drink to that!' You name it and Beau had it coming. If the old fool hadn't still been playing offstage romantic leads, a couple of otherwise fairly innocent people would still be alive today.* And a lot of others wouldn't still be haunted by nightmares. It served him right that his

* *Reel Murder.*

long-neglected wife had now asserted herself and was making him spend a small fortune on a round-the-world cruise. They were flying to join the *QE2* momentarily and Beau would be feeling far too poverty-stricken to pay out anything to Griselda, no matter how damning the stories she could tell.

Suddenly the front door slammed again.

'She hasn't come back?' Evangeline half-rose. 'Get rid of her, Trixie.'

I started for the door, only too willing. I'd had enough of Griselda, myself. I opened the door just as the hurrying footsteps reached it.

'It's all right,' I told Evangeline. 'It's only Martha.'

Evangeline snorted. It wasn't all right with her.

'Back already, darling?' I spoke quickly to cover Evangeline's rudeness. 'Where's Hugh?' The hallway behind her was empty.

'Don't mention that name!' Martha swept past me and fell on to the sofa in a miserable little heap.

'Darling!' I rushed over to her. 'What on earth—?'

'Oh, Mother, I've been a fool!' She sniffed back tears. I recognized that mood of old and braced myself.

'Every couple has little squabbles.' I tried to brace her, too. 'Especially just before a wedding. It doesn't mean a thing. Your nerves are strained, that's all—'

'There isn't going to *be* a wedding!'

CHAPTER 3

'Darling, what do you mean?'

'What have you done now, you idiot?' Evangeline demanded. 'If you've done anything to ruin our West End debut—'

'This has nothing to do with you,' Martha said. 'It's between Hugh and me. It was. It's over.'

'You've lost your mind,' Evangeline said. 'He was crazy over you. Or just crazy. Anyway, it was your last chance—and you've blown it. We might have known you would.'

'Evangeline—' I said between clenched teeth. 'Why don't you go and lie down and have your headache?'

'My head is clear as a bell right now,' Evangeline said. 'Unlike some others I could mention.'

'Evangeline—'

'I have come to my senses.' Martha threw back her head. 'The engagement was an aberration. A wild selfish notion. It won't happen again. I know my duty and I will do it.'

'What duty?' Evangeline asked suspiciously.

'Darling, perhaps *you* ought to lie down for a while—'

'No!' Martha surged to her feet, back straight, head high, an exalted light in her eyes: Joan of Arc going to the stake.

'No, Mother. I am going to stay here with you and take care of you for the rest of our lives.' She smiled seraphically at Evangeline. 'Both of you.'

Evangeline blanched. I didn't feel so well myself.

'Darling, no! We couldn't allow you to make such a sacrifice. You mustn't even think of it.'

'I'm determined.' Her chin rose higher, the flames were beginning to flicker in the straw at her feet now, but she was undaunted. 'I shall dedicate my life to making you happy. You and Aunt Vannie.'

'What did you call me?' Evangeline asked dangerously.

'Aunt Vannie.' For the first time, Martha's resolve wavered. 'I—I wanted a name of my own for you. Something nobody else ever called you before—'

Evangeline called Martha a name no one else had ever called her before.

'Evangeline—'

'But I always thought of you as Aunt Vannie—' Martha

quailed before the fury in Evangeline's eyes and wailed—
'I don't know *what* to call you—'

'Miss Sinclair will do.'

'EVANGELINE!'

'Now my head *is* aching,' Evangeline said accusingly.
'I'm going to go and lie down.' She refilled her brandy glass
and retired with injured dignity.

'Now, darling, what is all this? Sit down, I'm straining
my neck looking up at you.'

'Oh, Mother!' Martha sank back on to the sofa beside me
and hurled herself into my arms, knocking me backwards.
'Mother, I wish I was dead!'

'There, there, darling.' I struggled upright under her
weight and patted her shoulder. 'It can't be that bad. What's
happened?'

'It's Hugh!' she wailed.

'Yes . . .?' I had already figured that much out for myself.
'What about him? What has he done?'

'Married—' She sobbed incoherently into my bosom.
'Oh, Mother—he's been married before!'

'Hah!' There was a snort from the doorway. I might have
known it wouldn't be so easy to get rid of Evangeline. 'If he
hadn't been, at his age, you'd have a lot more to worry about.'

'Evangeline—*get out!*'

'I was just leaving—'

'And shut the door behind you!'

The door slammed.

'Just the same, she has a point, darling.' Heaven knew
we had seen some pretty ropey menages in our Hollywood
days. 'There's nothing in that to worry about—' A sudden
worry struck me. 'He *is* divorced, isn't he?'

'Ye-es . . .' Martha sniffled miserably. 'Yes, but she's still
around. She was there today . . .'

'Oh dear.' We'd seen that before, too: the complaisant
ex-wife and the legitimized mistress—and what Middle

America didn't know didn't hurt them. Of course, the studios had had the gossip writers on a tighter leash in those days. 'Still, that isn't necessarily so terrible . . .'

'There's worse!' Martha controlled herself with difficulty. 'Children—there are children! I'd be a stepmother! You'd be a grandmother!'

The door made a suspicious noise.

'Wait a minute, darling.' I set Martha to one side, rose, stalked over to the door and flung it open.

Evangeline was crouched outside, at keyhole level. She eyed my stormy face without a trace of guilt.

'I was looking for my lorgnette,' she announced majestically. It was a line from that Marx Brothers movie in which she replaced Margaret Dumont in the harried dowager role. Only they hadn't been able to harass Evangeline so easily. By the end of shooting, *they* were the ones on the verge of nervous breakdowns—all four of them.

'You don't *own* a lorgnette,' I snarled.

She shrugged and peered round me to offer more of her matchless words of wisdom to poor Martha.

'Anyone who waits until *your* age to marry must expect to be thrown in at the deep end.'

'Evangeline, suppose you go and lie down before I knock you down!'

'Don't worry, Mother.' Martha marched past us, a funeral procession of one on her way to the tumbril. '*I'm* going to lie down.' She burst into tears again and rushed across the hall, slamming the door of her room behind her. She never even noticed Gwenda, who had just descended the stairs, and nearly knocked her flying. She was the most promising of the theatrical kids who shared the maisonette at the top of the house but, if she didn't learn to change out of her tap shoes at the end of a practice session, she might not live long enough to fulfil that promise. She'd never have slipped so easily if she'd been wearing proper street shoes.

'Cwumbs!' Gwenda clung to the stair rail to catch her balance. 'What was that?'

'The lovebird,' Evangeline said. 'She's spent too much time cooing—and now the bill has come in.'

'Evangeline—' My warning was half-hearted. It was a pretty fair assessment of the situation.

'But what are you doing on the floor?' Gwenda let go of the railing and came over to us. 'Did she knock you down?'

'No such luck,' I said. We joined forces and got Evangeline on her feet again, still clutching her glass. She was so engrossed in her own thoughts, she hardly noticed us hoisting her up.

'Where have you been keeping yourself, my dear? Evangeline grasped Gwenda's arm firmly. 'We haven't seen nearly enough of you lately.'

'I've been wight here.' Gwenda looked startled, as well she might. I had been upstairs frequently, but Evangeline had never sought her company before.

'Never mind—' Evangeline was seeking it now. 'Come in and have a drink. You aren't in any hurry, are you?'

'Well . . .' Plainly, Gwenda was, but equally plainly, she was not going to miss an opportunity to get on a more social footing with Evangeline. 'P'waps, just a few minutes . . .'

'That's right. Just a drink and a friendly gossip.' Evangeline urged her into the living-room.

I was beginning to get it. This was going to be a discreet pumping session. It wasn't a bad idea. Gwenda must know more about Hugh and his situation than we did. That wouldn't be hard; obviously, we knew practically nothing.

'We're having brandy,' Evangeline said. 'Would you like some?'

'Oh, oh yes, thank you.' Gwenda wouldn't like it at all, but she was determined to be sophisticated if it killed her.

'There's sherry, too,' I suggested. 'Or gin and tonic.'

'P'waps a shewwy,' Gwenda said with relief.

I poured one for her and splashed more brandy into Evangeline's glass, then into my own. It was already growing dark outside, the early winter evening closing in with a hint of fog in the air. I moved around the living-room snapping on the table lamps to dispel the gloom. All the time, I kept wondering whether I should have gone to comfort Martha. Had she expected me to follow her when she dashed away so abruptly?

'Now, isn't this cosy?' Evangeline sipped her drink and beamed at Gwenda, who reacted with understandable nervousness. She wasn't accustomed to so much approval from Evangeline.

'How nice your hair looks.' Evangeline continued to overdo it. Not even Gwenda could believe that.

'Do you weally like it?' She raised one hand to poke uncertainly at the moth-eaten haystack that passed for her hair-do.

'Would I say so if I didn't?' That was a leading question. Evangeline would say anything that suited her game—especially if she was angling for something, which she was.

'Thank you.' Gwenda surrendered, still not quite believing it. She was right.

'Now, tell me—' The preliminaries over, Evangeline moved in for the kill. 'Tell me all about Hugh's ex-wife.'

'Do you mean Cwessida?' Gwenda wrinkled her brow.

'How many others were there?' I asked in sudden alarm. Martha really would go mad.

'Only Cwessida,' Gwenda said in surprise. 'But evewyone knows all about *her.*'

'We don't,' Evangeline said firmly. 'Maybe everyone in England does, but we're Americans, remember. We've walked in in the middle of the film.'

'Oh, wight . . .' But something was still puzzling Gwenda.

'And the children,' I said urgently. 'How many children are there? How old? What about *them?*'

'Oh, they're all wight.' Gwenda seemed relieved to be able to assure me. 'That is, Viola is all wight. Orlando can be a bit of a pain sometimes.'

'Orlando?'

'That's wight-*rrr*ight—' Gwenda was working to reverse the Edwardian accent she had previously worked so hard to acquire. It was still slipping all over the place, but she would manage perfectly well when she had lines to memorize and deliver.

'Cressida . . . Viola . . . Orlando . . .' Evangeline mused. 'Where were they all born—Stratford-on-Avon?'

'Just about,' Gwenda said. 'Crrressida's father was Sir Garrrick Errving—you *must* have heard of him—' She broke off, blushing fiercely. 'I'm sowwy. I mean, why ask me?'

'Sir Garrick Erving, the last of the Actor-Managers.' I identified him, sparing Evangeline's blood pressure. 'It's all right, Gwenda. Even I have heard of him.' Oh dear! Poor Martha was toiling along in frightfully illustrious footsteps. No wonder she had come down with buck fever.

'*Dear* Garrick!' Evangeline had identified him, too. 'How well I remember him. He was so kind during that Season I played in the West End before the War. Do you mean that sweet little golden-haired toddler he sometimes had with him was Hugh's wife? Surely she must have been—?'

'Oh yes, she was older than Hugh,' Gwenda said. 'But not so much older that she couldn't have children. They were her own, you know, not adopted—' Once more, she broke off and once more her face turned to fire. She tried to dowse it in her glass of sherry.

'Well, well, well.' Evangeline rose above all implications. 'Just imagine that. Small world, as they say. Little Cressida —Hugh's ex.'

'But I thought you knew,' Gwenda said innocently. 'I

mean, she's been in and out of here for the past couple of weeks. I was thinking how nice it was that you were all getting along so well together.'

'What?' Evangeline cried. 'You mean *that* Cressida is Cressie Nemo?'

'What Cressida?' I wanted to know. 'Who's Cressie Nemo?'

'Never mind,' Evangeline said quickly. 'I'll explain later.'

'What is there to explain?' That was even more ominous. 'Evangeline, what have you been up to?'

'Don't you know Cwessie Nemo, Twixie?' Gwenda was surprised. 'She's Widow's Mite Pwoductions.'

'Widow's Mite?' I repeated in disgust. 'It sounds like a branch of El Cheapo Productions.'

'It pwobably is.' Gwenda giggled. 'A feminist El Cheapo—'

'What a pity you can't stay longer, my dear.' Evangeline briskly pulled the welcome mat out from under Gwenda. 'You must come again when you're not so rushed.'

'Oh! Wight!' Looking slightly bewildered, Gwenda picked up her cue. 'I've got to meet Des . . . We're appearing at Leicester Square tonight.'

'The theatre?' Evangeline was learning.

'The tube station. See you later, Twixie.' Gwenda fled.

'OK.' I faced Evangeline sternly. 'Start talking!'

CHAPTER 4

'How was I to know?' For once, Evangeline was on the defensive. 'We never knew that Hugh had been married before. Even if we had known, I'd never have made the connection with Cressie. She's one of the embittered sort of feminists. Of course, having been married to Hugh would account for that.'

'Hugh is very nice.' I would not hear a word against my daughter's intended.

'If you like the dithering type. Although—' Evangeline decided to be gracious—'I can see that close association with Cressie might have undermined any man's confidence.'

'Faults on both sides, as usual—never mind about that. Just what are *you* doing with this Cressie? And how did you find her?'

'She contacted me. I got the sweetest letter after all that publicity last month. So friendly, so flattering, so—'

'The usual grovelling missive from somebody who wants something. We've all had plenty of those. What did this one want?'

'My help with her new project. My services actually—'

'Widow's Mite Productions.' It was all beginning to fall into place. I looked around the room for the script she had been flaunting earlier. What had she done with it? She had been holding it when Griselda rang the doorbell, then, by some sleight-of-hand, it had disappeared. She had been sheltering behind the armchair in the corner when Griselda entered . . . I started for the armchair.

'That's right.' Evangeline moved to intercept me. 'It's a new company—young vibrant, dedicated—'

'And broke,' I deduced. 'I take it the question of paying you hasn't actually been settled.'

'I don't need money.' That was true enough. 'And you must agree, Trixie, that we both have reached the age and stage when it behoves us to put back into Life something of the largesse we have received from it. After all,' she added slyly, 'you have your *own* little protégés upstairs.'

So that was it. Sheer jealousy had led her into getting mixed up with this bunch—and now whatever happened was going to be my fault.

'Those kids have talent,' I said.

'So have my kids.'

'Kids?' I scoffed. 'If Cressida was older than Hugh when she married him, that takes her out of the Young Talent bracket.'

'I am speaking in terms of the spirit, the freshness of approach, the enthusiasm . . .'

'Where is it?'

'They're seething with it! It oozes from every pore—'

'The script, I mean. Let's see this masterpiece they've conned you into making.' It must be around here somewhere, but I couldn't spot it.

'It *is* a masterpiece!' Evangeline swooped and retrieved the script from the middle of a pile of swatches of material heaped on the footstool. 'How can it be otherwise when it is based on a work by the greatest playwright in the world?'

'Anything *based on* can very easily be otherwise—' A sudden horrible thought struck me. What great playwright would Sir Garrick Erving's daughter be most likely to be pushing.

'Evangeline, tell me you don't mean Shakespeare.'

'Naturally I mean Shakespeare. And Lucy's adaptation is brilliant. It will become the most acclaimed film of our generation. It will soar above Orson's *Chimes at Midnight*, above Marlon's *Julius Cæsar*, above—'

'Don't keep me in suspense.' If only Hugh had been able to find a suitable theatre immediately, we'd now be settled down into a nice safe little West End run with *Arsenic and Old Lace*. I should have known that Evangeline, left alone and bored while Martha and I worked on the wedding plans, would get into mischief. 'Hit me with it.'

'It's the opportunity of a lifetime.' Evangeline was still doing the publicity routine. 'One of the great roles—'

I ran through as many as I could remember: Juliet,

Portia, Rosalind . . . Insane! Evangeline was fifty years too old for any of them. Sixty years. Of course, that had never stopped her yet.

'Evangeline—' I thought of something even more insane. '*Not* Cleopatra!'

'How sweet of you, Trixie.' She preened. 'We did discuss it. But, all things being equal—or unequal, really—we came to the conclusion that we wished to make a Statement relevant to the world as it exists today. Therefore, we are going to produce—*Queen Leah!*'

'Huh?' My knowledge of Shakespeare's plays was limited, but it wasn't that limited. 'Come again?'

'A Feminist version of *King Lear*.' Evangeline translated for me.

'Let me get this straight.' I couldn't believe it. I didn't want to believe it. '*You* are going to play King Lear. In drag.'

'Drag has nothing to do with it! Pay attention, Trixie!'

'I'm trying, but my brain's gone numb.'

'Lear has been rewritten as a woman. It becomes a metaphor for all that women have suffered in the male-dominated world. A searing indictment of man's inhumanity to woman. It will have more poignancy, power, drama, as—*Queen Leah!*'

She clasped the script to her bosom and raised her eyes to heaven, assuming the same pose she'd used in the final fadeout of *Love Lasts Forever*.

After a moment, my silence got to her. She lowered her gaze to my level and demanded, 'Well?'

'I'm speechless,' I admitted. 'But wait a minute, I'm working on it.'

'Don't bother! I might have known you wouldn't understand.'

'I understand that *King Lear* done from the woman's angle is going to turn out just like one of those 1940s womens' weepies. The ones that were so bad you refused them and they went to Joan Crawford instead.'

'Nonsense! You haven't got the picture at all.'

'And anyway—' I'd remembered a bit more of the plot. 'How can it be turned into such a great feminist statement about man's inhumanity to woman when it's the other way round? It's the old king's *daughters* who double-cross him and steal his kingdom. That makes them villainesses.'

'Oh, that—' Evangeline began to look vague. 'Well, in *this* script, the daughters are going to be sons—except for dear faithful Cordelia, of course.'

'I have heard of some hare-brained, ill-fated projects in my time in the business—but this one takes the cake!'

'I'm afraid your attitude simply proves how out-of-touch you are with truly modern trends and thinking.'

'Oh yeah? I can recognize a prime candidate for the Golden Turkey Awards when it flaps across my path. They'll be laughing at this one straight through to the Twenty-Second Century!'

The telephone rang abruptly and I snatched it up. 'Not now, Martha,' I said automatically. 'I'm too busy.'

'Oh—' a defeated voice said in my ear. 'She hasn't come home, then?'

'Oh, Hugh—' In the heat of the latest crisis, I had actually forgotten the earlier one.

'Trixie, I must speak to you. Then you can talk to Martha. Explain to her. She's got to understand. How soon can I see you?'

'You can't come here!' I said quickly.

'No, no. Certainly not. I quite understand. But I must see you—'

'Where are you? I'll go there.'

'I'm on my way to the Harpo Club. Come and have dinner with me there. It's in Fitzrovia, just off Charlotte Street. Any taxi-driver will know.'

'The Harpo Club,' I repeated dutifully. 'Just off Charlotte Street. I'll be there as fast as I can. I have to do a quick change first.'

'You're going to the Harpo Club?' Evangeline regarded me jealously. '*I* haven't been there yet.'

'Maybe you just don't know the right people.' I had no idea what the Harpo Club was but, since Evangeline clearly felt that it was a feather in my cap to be invited there, I wasn't going to admit it.

'Of course, Hugh must be a member.' Evangeline was still brooding. She'd loosened her hold on the script and, for a wild moment, I considered snatching it from her. But I didn't have time for a battle, Hugh would be waiting for me.

'I've got to change,' I said. 'Would you do me a favour and call for a taxi?'

'That won't be necessary,' she said smugly. 'Cressie is due at any moment. You can take her taxi.'

'Hugh's ex-wife is coming *here*?'

'And why not?'

'Martha—'

'Martha has undoubtedly sobbed herself to sleep by now. You know how these emotional scenes exhaust her. The girl has no stamina.'

'Not everyone can throw a tantrum on the hour, with matinees on the half-hour and encores on the quarter-hour.'

'Are you insinuating—?' Evangeline drew herself up.

'If the shoe fits!' I turned on my heel. 'I'll tell Martha I'm going out. Then she won't leave her room if she knows I'm not here.'

'Do you think that's wise?'

On second thought, I didn't. Martha would be sure to ask me where I was going and why. Worse, she might decide to come along with me if I didn't admit I was meeting

Hugh and she thought I was just going out to dinner in a restaurant. Then the fat would be in the fire.

'Cressie's been in and out of here several times without running into Martha. Let's just take our chances and trust to luck,' Evangeline urged. I hated to admit it, but she had a point.

'Well . . . I ought to hurry.' I moved quickly, spurred by the thought that this was going to be a good place to get out of—for a number of reasons. If Martha stayed in her room, Evangeline had got away with it. Again. But if Martha ventured out and discovered Cressida here, then I didn't want to be around for the fireworks. Furthermore, if I wasn't around, then Martha couldn't blame me for any of it. I hoped.

I came close to breaking my all-time record for the quick-change (twenty-two seconds, jumping out of a full 'career girl' business suit and into full evening dress with jewellery while the stage revolved to the Night Club set in *No Lady after Dark* on Broadway). My white and gold wool outfit wasn't nearly so elaborate, but then I didn't have two fitters standing by to shoehorn me into it, so I didn't break any records. I could hear a motor idling outside the house, so I dashed out of my room fastening my gold bracelet and with my ear-rings still clutched in one hand. I didn't want to lose that taxi. And, to tell the truth, I was dying to get a good look at Cressida.

Two minutes later, in the living-room, I was still dying to get a good look at Cressida. Oh, she stood there in front, of me all right—but she might as well have been wearing full camouflage gear. I mean, she was there—but she wasn't. She was a sort of amorphous blob.

The siren suit didn't help. It disguised any shape or form she might have had. She was obviously anti-make-up, which was a pity. She was the sort of woman make-up had been invented for. Her pale beige eyebrows faded into her pale beige face, her eyelashes were insignificant, if not actually non-existent, and her thin formless lips blurred into the surrounding beige.

Max Factor, Elizabeth Arden, Percy Westmore, Helena Rubinstein—thou shouldst be here at this hour. That face cried out for every available artifice. And at least a double set of false eyelashes.

'Trixie Dolan?' The pale beige gaze swept me up and down as Evangeline introduced us. She wasn't impressed, either. 'Oh, yes, the . . . comedienne.'

'Ms Nemo?' I batted it back to her. 'The . . . er . . . I'm afraid I don't know *your* work.' But I knew her type: Life was Real, Life was Earnest—and anybody who could lighten the load with a few laughs wasn't really playing fair.

'The taxi is waiting, Trixie,' Evangeline said nervously. Every now and again she gets worried about what I might say. 'You don't want to be late for . . . your appointment.'

'That's right. I must dash.' I began backing out, just in case that fatal word 'Hugh' escaped any unwary lips. 'I don't want to lose that taxi.'

'You won't,' Cressida said coldly. 'Nova will wait.'

'That's good,' I said. 'But I don't want to put anybody to any extra trouble.' I beamed a smile to a pleasant-looking little woman in the corner. Nobody had bothered to introduce her, which probably meant that she was the writer. Along with Shakespeare. But she wasn't whirling in her grave—not yet.

'Goodbye, Trixie,' Evangeline said firmly. I took the hint and left.

The taxi was waiting at the foot of the steps. Vaguely, I noticed that it was one of the cabs that had sold their plain black panels for advertising. I got in, scarcely bothering to glance at the gaudy slogan.

'Harpo Club, please,' I directed. 'It's just off—'

'I know where it is.' Why should I be surprised to find

that the driver was a woman? They were even driving London buses these days—although not many of them.

'It's a nice place. They have good food.' She was obviously as chatty as some of her male counterparts, but a little careless. She had forgotten to put down the flag to start the meter running.

'Your flag,' I prompted, trying to make myself comfortable. Something long and hard seemed to be wedged between the cushions at my back. I probed for it.

'What flag?' She seemed puzzled.

'Your meter—it's not running. You've forgotten to start it.'

'Oh, that!' She laughed. 'You don't think we'd charge *you*, do you?' She laughed some more. 'You don't think this is a working taxi, do you?'

'I guess not.' By this time, I didn't. The source of my discomfort, when dislodged, proved to be a zoom lens. At the same moment, I recalled the reels of film painted on the door panels, the film streeling out to spell WMP. 'This taxi belongs to Widow's Mite Productions, then?'

'Makes much more sense than a van driving around town,' she said. 'You can pile a lot of equipment into it, more comfortable riding for the players—and the great plus: you can drive down all the streets that are blocked off to commercial vehicles and private cars. There are a lot of them now—too many—only open to buses and taxis. Makes getting around town a lot easier.'

'I hadn't thought of that.' I'd never had reason to, but I didn't add that. 'What happens if you get caught?'

'Don't know. It hasn't happened yet. But I don't see what they could do about it. We have our logo in plain sight, so we're not really trying to pass ourselves off as a taxi. We just happen to have started out as one.'

'That's true . . .' But I wouldn't like to hear her try to argue it before a judge. That *we* was making me nervous, too. It was beginning to sound as though she and the taxi were an inseparable unit.

We—I mean *they*—jumped a red light, veered across a line of traffic, escaped a boring bottleneck by taking a short cut up a bus lane, cut across another line of traffic and plunged into a maze of little crooked streets that would have done credit to a mediæval town—and possibly had. They were uneven enough to be cobblestoned, but I think it was mostly potholes.

'Here we are,' Nova said finally and I opened my eyes.

We had stopped in front of a recessed doorway. It didn't look like much but, as I watched, several obviously theatrical types entered, so it must be the right place.

'Want me to wait for you?' my driver offered.

'Oh, no—no, thanks,' I said hurriedly. 'I'll be here quite a while. I'm having dinner with a friend.'

'I could come back and pick you up later. Both of you.'

'That's very kind, but you mustn't bother.' I couldn't go through that again. 'I'm sure he'll drive me home himself.'

CHAPTER 5

Hugh was seated alone at a table—and it wasn't his first drink. 'Trixie—so good of you to come.' He stumbled to his feet. 'Sit down. Have a drink.'

'Hugh, my dear.' I moved my cheek so that it connected with his badly-aimed kiss. 'Do sit down.' *Before you fall down.*

'Yes . . .' He waved his hand and a hovering waiter appeared beside us with a menu. Instantly. I couldn't help being impressed. Hugh had spent so much time kowtowing to Evangeline—yes, and to me, too—when we first met that it was still startling to realize just how important he was in his own world.

The fawning waiter provided fresh evidence of that importance. Frantic customers at another table were trying to call him but—obviously a 'resting' actor, as are most of the waiters in New York—he was not to be torn from Hugh's side so easily. He turned his back to the other table and beamed at me; it seemed that I was basking in Hugh's reflected glory.

'The Coquilles St Jacques are very good tonight,' he confided. 'And the Tournedos Rossini—'

'I'll have another drink,' Hugh said abruptly. 'Trixie?'

'A medium sherry, please.' I looked at Hugh's unhappy face. 'A large one.'

'Right away, Miss Dolan,' he assured me. 'Right away, Mr Carpenter.' He didn't want Hugh to feel left out. Nodding emphatically to assure us of his good will, he dashed away. Someone at an adjoining table made a tentative grab at his coat-tail, but he was too fast for them.

'How is Martha?' Hugh reminded me that I had troubles of my own.

'Upset.' That was putting it mildly. Who said only the English were experts at understatement?

'I was afraid of that.' He sighed deeply. 'Perhaps I should have broken it to her more gently, but I had no idea she thought . . .'

'It's hard to know what Martha is thinking sometimes.' And that was another understatement in the grand manner.

'Here we are!' The waiter had broken all records—for us.

'Thank you . . . Trevor.'

'Oh! You know my name!' He was thrilled.

'I took a wild guess.' Guided by the plaintive cries from the other tables, it wasn't hard. 'You seem to be in great demand.'

'Oh, you can ignore them. They just want attention.' He dabbed at an imaginary crumb on the tablecloth and confided, 'The Noisettes d'Agneau are sheer heaven to-night.'

'They sound great.' If anyone ever got them. A rhythmic drumming was coming from a corner table where a desperate would-be diner had picked up knife and fork and gone into a Gene Krupa routine. He had no other use for the implements.

'Don't let us keep you,' I said. 'Your other tables seem anxious to talk to you.'

'They can wait. I've never had a chance to talk to *you* before, Miss Dolan. I'd just like to tell you how much I loved all your films. Can we hope for a Season at the National Film Theatre or the Silver Screen in the Sky?'

'Well, nothing definite has been decided yet,' I said modestly. I had a lot to be modest about; the subject had never even been mentioned by those prestige venues. But perhaps Beau's arm could be twisted . . . when he returned from his trip.

'There's Job Farraday,' Hugh said abruptly, nodding to someone.

'Good Lord! Is he still around?' I turned and waved behind me automatically. 'I'd heard he transferred his operations over here about the time of the McCarthy Hearings—' A lot of them had. Job Farraday wasn't quite up in the ranks of the Hollywood Ten, nor even the first couple of hundred. In fact, there was a nasty rumour that he wasn't even a fellow-traveller, but had taken advantage of the situation to slip away from impending bankruptcy under the guise of being forced into exile and political martyrdom. He had never returned and, to tell the truth, none of us had missed him, although he had been responsible for many fine B pictures in his time, some of which had attained cult status in the intervening years.

'Trixie Dolan—as I live and almost breathe!' Job rushed

over to us. I was engulfed in a bear hug and overwhelmed by the miasma of menthol. eucalyptus oil and whatever herbal remedies he was indulging in at the moment. 'Trixie —more beautiful than ever!'

'Job, darling, you haven't changed a bit!' It was true. He had looked a beat-up sixty forty years ago and he looked a beat-up sixty now. With that kind of face, a few more wrinkles and a bit more rumpling didn't make any difference. 'How are you?'

'My doctor says I should have died ten years ago, but I'm going to make it through tonight just to spite him. Seeing you helps. You're a sight for sore eyes—and my eyes aren't what they used to be, either.'

'They never were, Job,' I reminded him. Job had been one of the greatest hypochondriacs in an industry notorious for the number of its neurotics and the inventiveness of its hypochondriacs. There was more truth than poetry in the story of the director who indiscriminately sampled everyone else's pills (although generously passing round his own) having lunch with a writer who had carelessly set down a pill bottle beside his plate. The director had eagerly shaken out a couple of the pills and swallowed them before thinking to ask, 'What are those for?' 'The dog,' the writer answered. 'I've just come from the vet's. But cheer up, you'll never get distemper.' The story hadn't actually been told about Job, but it very well could have been.

'Have a drink, Job.' Hugh bowed to the inevitable. 'What would you like?'

'I'd like the Elixir of Youth,' Job said, 'but I'll settle for a double Scotch with Scottish spring water.'

'Right away, Mr Farraday,' Trevor carolled, and skipped off to run the gauntlet between his tables of disgruntled customers.

'You're doing very well here, Job,' I deduced, taking my cue from Trevor's attitude.

'I can't complain. Well, I could, but who would believe me? Things have been worse, a lot worse.'

'You're casting for a new show, I hear,' Hugh said.

'*Robin Hood*, a musical. But I'm having a lot of trouble getting the Merry Men together. Not many actors can handle a bow and arrow. I'm sending the ones I've got so far to archery lessons, but they're still a danger to the audience and each other. We may have to rewrite some scenes so they just gesture with the bows and arrows.'

'A musical Robin Hood.' Hugh frowned thoughtfully, then seemed struck by sudden alarm. 'You're not reviving *Twang!*, are you?'

'No, no, this is a completely new show. Great book, great music, fantastic scenic effects—showers of arrows arching across the stage like a rainbow. Maybe I can hire the Olympic Archery Team—if they've got one—to stand in the wings and shoot the arrows while the actors mime.'

'What a pity you couldn't get my daughter to help out—' I seldom resisted the chance to brag about Martha's accomplishments. 'Archery is one of her hobbies. She won a gold medal for it at school. But—' I dashed the hope beginning to dawn on Job's face—'she wouldn't be interested. She hates show business.'

'Your drink, Mr Farraday.' Trevor set it down in front of him and added a bowl of salted almonds and cashews. Behind him, one table stood up and mimed putting on their coats.

'Perhaps Trevor is good at archery,' I suggested. Being a waiter certainly wasn't one of his accomplishments.

'Oh yes. Yes, I am. How clever of you to guess, Miss Dolan.' He was obviously lying in his teeth. He'd probably be even more of a danger than the actors Job had already hired. I began to wish I hadn't been so flip in my suggestions.

'You can do archery?' Job had his doubts, too, but if you're not an optimist there's no point in being in this game. 'You're sure?'

'I can show you the medal *I* won for it at school.'

'I'd rather see you in action.' Job took out a card and scribbled something on it. 'Come round to the Delphic tomorrow afternoon. Bring your own bow and arrows. We'll give you an audition.'

'Wonderful! But . . .' Trevor hesitated. 'Could we make it Monday afternoon? I'm supposed to go home for the weekend. I'll have to—' he added, in a burst of inspiration —'my archery equipment is there.'

'OK, Monday afternoon.' Job nodded and I could foresee a busy weekend for Trevor as he went out and bought the equipment and spent the weekend learning to use it. But first . . .

'Don't you think you ought to attend to your other tables?' I asked.

I turned and waved a hand to indicate them, just in case he had forgotten where they were. 'Oh-oh!'

'Oh-oh!' Job echoed as he saw the woman standing in the doorway. 'There's my dinner date.'

Just in case anyone had missed her entrance, Griselda took a step backwards and treated them to her favourite pose.

'You gotta admit it,' Job said with reluctant admiration. 'She can still fill a doorway.'

Even the customers at Trevor's tables had stopped baying for his blood and were staring at her in bemusement.

Then there was a murmur of recognition and a spatter of applause. Griselda dropped the pose and moved forward, one step ahead of a waiter with a loaded tray who had been trying to get past her. She didn't move far; she spotted Job at our table and stopped short. Then she spotted me.

We bared our teeth at each other and she stayed where she was, which was fine with me. After a moment she began to tap her foot.

'So long, Trixie,' Job sighed. 'I'll see you later. 'Bye, Hugh.' He heaved himself to his feet and went to claim his prize.

I watched him thoughtfully as he hugged Griselda—with somewhat less warmth than he had hugged me—and led her to his table. Job Farraday . . . wasn't there some genuine scandal in his dim and distant past? Something nastier than money or politics? I couldn't quite remember. I'd have to ask Evangeline, her elephantine memory went a lot farther back than mine.

'Trixie—' Hugh began, then noticed that Trevor was still hovering and changed what he had been going to say. 'Shall we order now?'

'The lamb,' I said quickly. He was right. We had to order while we still had Trevor's undivided attention. Someone more important might come in as the restaurant filled up and then we'd join the other brooding nonentities who were eyeing us jealously from the surrounding tables. If we actually got served before they did, I was afraid they might form themselves into a lynch mob.

As he ordered, Hugh seemed to become aware of the general unrest for the first time. He looked around absently and suggested, 'Perhaps you ought to take care of the other tables when you've finished here, Trevor.'

'If you say so, Mr Carpenter.' Trevor's tone implied that Hugh's judgement was at fault, but a loyal subaltern would obey the order, even unto the Valley of Death.

From the look of the disgruntled diners, that Valley was pretty close. Trevor waved a *Wait a minute, can't you?* to them as he sped towards the kitchen with our order. Several of them transferred their attention to us then.

'Trixie—' Oblivious to all, Hugh leaned forward

earnestly. 'Trixie, you've got to help me. Martha says it's all over. It can't be. I've just found her. I love her. I thought she loved me. We can sort it out. If only she'll talk to me—'

'Martha has had a shock, I'm afraid. She hadn't realized that you'd been married before. Or that there were children involved.'

'It's all my fault,' he abased himself. 'I should have broken it to her earlier. Especially about the children.'

'I don't think Martha has ever seen herself as the motherly type,' I said truthfully.

'But with your example—' He broke off. 'Perhaps blood *will* out,' he said bitterly.

'Look, you haven't given poor Martha time to come to terms with all this,' I said desperately. I didn't want her to lose him. 'After all, she only learned about it—when? A few hours ago? Give her a bit more time.'

'You're right,' he said abjectly. 'You're so right, Trixie. That's why I needed to talk to you. You're calmer. You can, I hope, see both sides of this objectively.'

'I think I can.' I could certainly see that the invitations had already gone out. 'And I'm very fond of you both. I want what's best for you . . .' Out of the corner of my eye, I saw the occupants of a nearby table rise and head towards us *en bloc*. Their determined strides put me off my own. Were they going to wreak their revenge on us for Trevor's neglect?

'I hoped you'd feel like that.' Hugh did not seem to notice that I had faltered to a halt—or why. 'Explain to Martha, tell her I'm not totally unfeeling. I had no idea that Cressida was going to be there this afternoon. I'd have arranged quite a different meeting for them, in a more civilized setting, at a better time.'

'Yes,' I said weakly, hoping the Harpo was sufficiently civilized to preclude the scene I feared. The elderly man in the lead carried a walking stick with a silver knob heavy enough to qualify it as a blunt instrument. The two middle-aged men and a woman following immediately behind him looked furious enough to use it as such if he didn't. I began to revise my first impression; Trevor alone could not account for all this hostility. They all looked vaguely familiar; perhaps, if they'd been wearing pleasanter expressions, I might have been able to identify them.

'Hugh,' their leader said in a Voice of Doom, 'we'd like a word with you.'

'Sure.' I started to get up. 'I'll just go and powder my nose.' Hugh's feet crushed down on mine, anchoring me to the floor.

'Trixie is part of the family,' he said. 'You can talk in front of her.'

I could have done without the vote of confidence. Whatever they had to say was obviously no business of mine—and I didn't want to make it my business.

'Trixie—' But I didn't have a choice. Hugh began the introductions, first indicating the elder statesman. 'Have you met Roger Thor?'

'We haven't met.' I recognized him now. 'But I've admired your work so much, Mr Thor.'

'And I yours.' He shook hands, his expression becoming more social. 'Do call me Roger.'

'And Posy Miller, the designer.' They were either being introduced in order of importance or Hugh was reverting to normal social precedence after beginning with the obvious leader of the pack.

'Of course.' I smiled warmly at Posy Miller, although there was no 'of course' about it. The name rang a faint distant bell, that was all. Not in the Motley, Messel or Beaton class.

'And Clive Anderson and Whitby Grant.'

Again the names rang faint bells, as did the now pleasant

faces. The social smiles didn't last very long, though. As soon as the handshaking was over, the faces resumed their grim expressions.

'Sit down,' Hugh suggested, without any real hope of their doing so. For one thing, there weren't enough chairs. For another, you can't conduct a Grand Scene from a sitting position—and that was clearly what they intended.

'I think you know the problem, Hugh.' Roger Thor fired the opening shot.

'I've heard rumours.' Hugh wriggled uneasily. 'But I don't see what I can do about it.'

'You can talk to her—make her see reason.'

'See reason?' Hugh gave a hollow laugh. 'Cressida divorced me five years ago. She wouldn't listen to anything I said then and she isn't going to listen now. Posy would have a better chance of persuading her than I would.'

'Include me out!' Posy said. 'I tried to talk to her last week. She told me I was an Uncle Tomming cow and hung up on me. I was glad I'd used the telephone. If we'd been face-to-face, she might have assaulted me.'

'No, really—' Hugh winced. 'She isn't that bad.' But the hangdog look in his eyes said that she was.

'Please, Hugh.' Clive Anderson did the both-hands-on-the-table-leaning-forward-earnestly bit, to stare intently into Hugh's shifting eyes. 'You're our last hope. You've got to help us.'

'I would if I could.' Hugh shied back nervously as Whitby Grant also took up the half-threatening, half-imploring position. 'But nothing I could say would influence her. You know how she is.'

There were glum nods all around. They knew how she was.

'There must be something you can do,' Whitby Grant insisted. 'Cut off her alimony—'

'And she'd cut off my access to the children!' If she didn't cut off something worse. I was beginning to see why Martha looked so good to him.

'She's no better than a thief!' Clive was getting even more agitated. 'She's stealing our work, our talent—our nest-egg. It's robbery! Sheer robbery!'

'In fact, highway robbery,' Posy said. 'Very fitting—for a Highwayman.'

'You can laugh!' Clive snapped. 'They're not *your* residuals!'

'Children, children . . .' Roger Thor raised his hands to heaven and then let them fall, one each, on the shoulder of the two men hunched over the table. 'Let us not quarrel among ourselves. We must not be sidetracked. And Posy —' he lowered his head at her—'try to control your natural mischievousness. This is neither the time nor place for it. The matter is too serious for frivolity.'

And then I had him! The Highwayman! Fifteen years ago . . . no, perhaps more like twenty. How time flies! But, yes, it was all coming back to me now. Roger Thor as *The Highwayman*. The silhouette in greatcoat, tricorne hat and lace jabot brooding behind the title credits of one of TV's first big international hit series.

And that was why the others were so familiar, too. Clive Anderson had been the juvenile lead, the heroine's rakehell kid brother, always getting into scrapes. I took another incredulous look at his collection of lines and wrinkles; either that series had been even longer than twenty years ago, or he'd been raking a lot more hell in his private life since then.

Whitby Grant had been the Highwayman's faithful servant, who doubled for his master when the Highwayman was required elsewhere, which happened often enough to qualify him as second lead.

Posy Miller, of course, had been responsible for those fabulous sets and even more fabulous costumes.

'Of course, *The Highwayman*!' I blurted out. 'That was

such a wonderful series. I don't know why they don't re-release it. There's a whole new audience out there now. They'd love it!'

Hugh groaned and buried his face in his hands.

CHAPTER 6

So there I was with my foot in my mouth. Again. All four feet, in fact—and, believe me, I was the dumb bitch with the mouth big enough. They stared at me with varying degrees of hostility.

'Dear lady—' Finally, Roger spoke. 'That is precisely what we are trying to arrange.'

I waited, chewing on a toe or two and trying to look sympathetic, if not intelligent. There was no help forthcoming from Hugh; he just sat there as though waiting for the next blow to fall.

It was beginning to make sense—or almost. I wasn't going to open my mouth again, but I risked raising my eyebrows questioningly.

'I don't believe she knows what we're talking about!' Posy cried.

I nodded my head, then shook it, still trying to look hopefully questioning. It worked. Too well. Everybody around us was beginning to stare. I realized that I had inadvertently been giving a very fair imitation of the late lamented Harpo and people were starting to think that I was part of the floor show.

'Doesn't she?' Roger frowned. 'Haven't you told her, Hugh?'

'I was going to mention it,' Hugh mumbled. 'But then you burst in on us and I hadn't the chance.'

'Mention what?' I found my voice again.

'This . . . additional problem. And why Martha needn't be jealous.'

'Tell me now,' I suggested. 'It sure doesn't seem to be any great secret. I must be the only one who doesn't know.'

'It was in *The Stage* last week,' Clive said accusingly.

'I haven't even seen *Variety* since I've been here.' I fought back. 'Life has been too hectic.'

No one could argue with that. I followed up my advantage immediately. 'This has something to do with Cressida, I gather.'

'*Everything* to do with Cressida!' Whitby Grant snarled.

Hugh winced again. There was still no help coming from that quarter.

'She is blocking the re-release of the series,' Roger said. 'We all had that clause in our contracts, but she is the only one invoking it. Because of her objections, *The Highwayman* cannot ride again.'

'What business is it of hers?' I was bewildered.

'She played the Lady Jessamyn. And she was delighted with the role when she needed the money. Now she is claiming that the depiction of the character infringes her present dignity and beliefs. She is afraid that she will not be taken seriously in her new incarnation if the ghost of her past indiscretion is paraded across the screens in the present climate. She is, in short, mad. And her madness is about to cost the rest of us a small fortune.'

'*Cressida* was the Lady Jessamyn?' It was all coming back to me and it was a good thing I was sitting down or I'd be reeling. That—that faceless scarecrow in overalls had been the Lady Jessamyn? The Highwayman's Lady, who spent most of the episodes falling out of her decolletage in the eighteenth-century sequences and barely covered by her miniskirt in the modern sequences, so that the viewers got the best of both worlds as the action swerved between the present and the ghostly past for reasons too complicated to grasp easily. Whenever the action flagged, Lady Jessamyn had slipped into something comfortable, like bra and scanties, and cavorted around the lavish sets with either the Highwayman or his faithful valet pretending to be him. (The viewer had often got the impression that Lady Jessamyn's costume might usefully have included a pair of glasses.)

'Oh, she's recanted now,' Posy said. 'Actually, she's worked up quite a good act about the way she was taken advantage of and exploited in her ignorant youth before the scales dropped from her eyes. We don't mind that, but when she invokes that clause in the contract to block the re-runs, it hits the rest of us financially—and it hits us hard. And all because she wants to be taken seriously.'

'Seriously . . .' I echoed faintly. Cressida was planning to star Evangeline as *King Lear* and she expected to be taken seriously? What was left of my mind settled down to some serious boggling.

'I'm sorry,' Hugh said miserably. 'If only there were something I could do . . .' He brightened. 'Look, Job Farraday is over there and he's casting for his new *Robin Hood*. You've all done lots of costume work. Why don't you speak to him? Roger, you'd make a terrific Sheriff of Nottingham. Clive, I can see you as Will Scarlet. And Whit, Posy—I'm sure he could find something for you. It won't help about the residuals, but it would be a bird in the hand. Would you like me to have a word with him?'

'Don't worry about me,' Posy said. 'I'm already involved in that show. Wait until you see my Clearing in Sherwood Forest.'

'There's only one person we want you to have a word with,' Whitby Grant said with an odd air of menace.

'Sorry.' Hugh shook his head. 'It's hopeless, Whit. I don't even know where Cressida is right now.'

'As a matter of fact—' my mouth was beginning to feel

lonely without all those feet in it—'she's back at the house. At least, she was when I left.'

'Cressida?' Hugh lurched to his feet, nearly demolishing mine in the process. 'At the house? With Martha?'

'Not necessarily,' I said. 'She's having a script conference with Evangeline. If we're lucky, Martha will stay in her room—' I gave him a meaningful look—'weeping into her pillow.'

'Oh God!' Hugh was distraught. 'My poor Martha! Why didn't you tell me? They mustn't meet!'

'Here we are.' Trevor appeared with a laden tray. 'And I must say the chef has outdone himself. All because he wants your autograph. You will give it to him, won't you, Miss Dolan?'

'No time for that!' Hugh grabbed my arm and tried to pull me to my feet. 'We must be going.'

'I'm hungry,' I protested, refusing to be budged. 'You go ahead. I'll meet you there later. After I eat.'

'We'll *all* go ahead,' Roger said. 'What did you say the address was?'

I hadn't said and, after one look at Whitby's face, I wasn't going to. 'Oh, Trevor, what a good suggestion you gave me! That looks delicious. Of course I'll give the chef my autograph. How kind of him to ask.'

'Trixie—' Hugh looked at the others, still waiting to learn where Cressida could be found, and changed his mind. We couldn't lead them to her in the mood they were in. 'Perhaps you're right.' He sat down again. 'It can wait until we've had our meal.'

'Where is she?' Roger Thor demanded; his knuckles were white against the glittering silver knob of his walking stick.

'She'll have gone by now, anyway,' I said. 'She kept her taxi waiting outside.' I decided not to mention that I had used it to get here.

'Perhaps we ought to have a word with Job—' Clive

Anderson wavered. 'It can't do any harm to remind him that we're well-seasoned character actors experienced in costume work.'

'Well . . .' Roger Thor hovered irresolutely as the others moved off towards Job's table. 'Do your best, Hugh, won't you?'

'You know I will,' Hugh said, grasping the outstretched hand.

Griselda glared at them as they approached to break up her tête-à-tête, but Job greeted them with what appeared to be relief. It was a shame that we were too far away to overhear the ensuing conversation, but it looked lively and promising. Griselda seemed to grow more annoyed by the minute; she hated not being the centre of attention. Perhaps she ought to go back to the doorway and do her thing again.

'Trixie—' Hugh was just toying with his Dover sole, his mind on other matters. 'Trixie, are you sure there's no possibility they might meet?'

'Don't worry.' I was already doing enough worrying for both of us. 'Evangeline will keep them apart.' Unless her warped sense of humour got the better of her and she decided it might be more amusing to throw them together and see what happened. Hugh would be happier if he didn't suspect that, though.

'I wouldn't want Martha to be hurt,' he said. 'And I want this wedding to go ahead. She didn't really mean it when she called it off, did she?'

'I hope not,' I said fervently. The thought of Martha as a prop for my declining years was already sending me into a decline. 'I'll talk to her in the morning when the shock has had time to wear off a bit.'

'Oh.' He was downcast. 'I was rather hoping that, er, I might be able to see her when I took you home.'

'You can try but, if I know Martha, she's taken a sleeping pill or two. She won't be wakeable until morning.'

'Oh. Er, actually, I wouldn't mind having a word with Cressida, either. If she's still there, that is.'

'Oh, good! You *are* going to try to persuade her to let them re-release *The Highwayman*.' Hugh would know how important residuals were to the actors, of course. Come to think of it, I hadn't seen any of them in anything recently. Although Roger Thor probably had enough socked away to keep him in reasonable comfort for the rest of his life, there was something about the two younger men that suggested a battle to keep on the right side of shabby gentility. And even though Posy Miller's name appeared fairly regularly in television credits, it would do no harm at all for *The Highwayman* to remind the world of her dazzling early success; it would undoubtedly lead to more commissions.

'Er, I'm not sure about that. One has to judge the time and temper—especially the temper—before making so bold. We have other business to discuss, however, and it can be rather hard to get hold of Cressida. She moves about a lot.'

I nodded sympathetically, mentally translating that into: 'No fixed address'. From what I had seen of it, I suspected that Widow's Mite was some sort of no-budget collective, probably moving from place to place as they wore out their welcome among their supporters.

'She *has* a house,' Hugh said bitterly. 'She just doesn't stay in it. She'd rather hare all over the city with that rag-taggle-and-bob lot she's mixed up with. I wouldn't even mind if they all moved into the house, if that's the way she wants it, but she says it's too far out in the country. We bought it in the country especially because we thought it would be a good place to bring up the children. Now I never know where *they* are, either!'

'I see.' And I didn't like what I was beginning to see. It was as well I'd almost finished my delicious meal because I had abruptly lost my appetite.

'Ready for your sweet?' Hugh had never had any appetite for his own meal, now he raised his hand and Trevor aimed the sweets trolley at us.

'I've had enough,' I said. 'If you want coffee, why don't we have it back at the house?'

'Good.' His face cleared slightly and he told Trevor, 'Just the bill, please.'

'But I was going to recommend the profiteroles,' Trevor protested. 'Chef has outdone himself. You must taste them.'

'You can eat my share,' I said quickly as Hugh's face darkened again. I gathered up my handbag and bits and bobs. 'Just see us to the door first, will you, Trevor?'

'Of course, Miss Dolan.' He pulled back my chair.

'This should cover it.' Hugh dropped a few banknotes on the table, unwilling to wait any longer. 'Never mind the change.'

'Oh, thank you, Mr Carpenter!' Trevor swept it up and followed us to the door, bowing all the way, in the best flunkey tradition. Everyone watched our progress, wondering just how much Hugh *had* tipped.

'Well—' I turned and stretched out one hand to Trevor. 'Goodbye and thank you for taking such good care of us.'

'Come again, *please*.' Trevor, the perfect patsy, shook my hand vigorously.

I did my sleight-of-hand and a cascade of silverware clattered noisily to the floor. If they want to call a place after Harpo, I can go along with a gag.

'Oh, Miss Dolan—' Trevor was overcome with delight. 'You're perfect!'

'Nonsense!' I said throatily. 'Nobody's perfect!' I turned and swung out with a Mae West twitch of the hips. As I did so, I let the *Reserved* table notice fall behind me.

I exited on a wave of applause—much louder than Griselda had got—and laughter. One hand on hip, I did a Betty Grable backward glance and happily saw that

Griselda was spitting blood at being upstaged. Hugh's face was crimson, whether with embarrassment or laughter, I couldn't tell. But it was worth it.

'Don't you want to take a bow?' Hugh muttered, slipping his hand under my elbow.

'It would be an anti-climax.' I hurried through the little reception area. 'Never spoil a good exit.'

'And always leave them laughing!' Hugh was laughing now. Thank heavens he wasn't annoyed with me. 'That exit should feature in a few gossip columns tomorrow. Good publicity for the show when it opens.' He raised his hand and hailed a passing taxi. I was relieved to see that it was a genuine taxi and not the Widow's Mite vehicle.

'Since you mention it—' I settled back as we drove off, passing a taxi parked at the end of the street which looked uneasily familiar—'I've been meaning to ask: when *are* we going to open? We haven't even gone into rehearsal yet.'

'I'm still trying to find a theatre,' Hugh said. 'Not many are dark at the moment—and it has to be the right one. We couldn't put you into one so big that you'd rattle around and be lost on an enormous stage. We want something smaller, intimate—'

'Yes, but when will we get it? When, Hugh?'

'Soon, I hope. Be patient. There's no great urgency, is there? You're happy here, aren't you? Having a good holiday? Enjoying yourself?'

'I'm all right, but Evangeline is getting bored. And that means she's getting into trouble. Before you have any of your famous words with anyone else, you might try to talk some sense into Evangeline.'

'What's the matter?' Hugh sounded fearful. 'What trouble?'

'The worst.' I confirmed his every fear. 'She's about to make an almighty fool of herself. Permanently—on film.

After spending a lifetime building up a reputation to be proud of, she's going to blow it sky-high. Her name will be a laughing-stock—'

'Come now, it can't be that bad,' Hugh said uneasily. 'After all, a lifetime's reputation can't be erased by one mistake.' He did not sound entirely convinced.

'It depends on the mistake—and Evangeline is hellbent on a lulu! Would you believe it—she wants to play *King Lear*?'

'*King Lear*?' Hugh echoed blankly. 'Are you sure? I mean, you're not having me on, are you?'

'Would I joke about a thing like that? She's fallen into the clutches of some maniac feminist film group—' I broke off, suddenly remembering whose ex-wife was leading the maniacs.

'Before you say anything more, Trixie—' Hugh's voice was strangulated. 'Perhaps I ought to tell you. I'm backing Cressida's new film.'

We rode quite a long way in total silence.

'I suppose there's no point in asking this—' I found my voice again—'but are you out of your mind?'

'Not yet,' Hugh said grimly. 'I wouldn't take any bets about the future, though. Believe me, Trixie, I didn't know what the film was going to be.'

'Now that you know—' Hope glimmered brightly at the end of a dark tunnel—'you can withdraw the financing, can't you?'

'No,' Hugh said flatly.

'Don't speak so fast—you haven't heard all of it.' I was sure I could convince him. 'It won't be nearly such a good script as the real *King Lear*. They're rewriting it from a feminist standpoint. *King Lear* is making a sex change to *Queen Leah*. Can you imagine what the critics will say about that?'

Hugh could. He groaned.

'And Regan and Goneril are being rewritten as male roles—'

I could feel Hugh flinch.

'It's going to be a mess, Hugh. A shambles. And you could stop it so easily. No money, no film, no lost reputations. Just remember, it won't do your own reputation any good to be caught financing a turkey like that. And you've got a lot longer to try to live it down than Evangeline has.' I glanced sideways at him as we passed a streetlamp to see how I was doing. His eyes were closed and his lips were moving silently. Maybe he was praying. Or cursing.

'You can do it, Hugh.' I pressed home my advantage. 'Just—'

'I can't,' Hugh groaned. 'Don't you understand? If I withdraw my financial support, Cressida will withdraw my access to the children.'

'She can't do that!' I remembered Cressida's grim humourless face and changed my mind. 'Well, she can't get away with it. You can go to Court and force her—'

'No!' Hugh stiffened. 'Once was enough! I can't go through that again. I couldn't put the children through it again.'

'I see.' I let the temperature drop below freezing. 'Tell me one thing, Hugh. Are you marrying Martha just to acquire a suitable stepmother for your children?'

'God!' Hugh looked at me aghast. 'No wonder poor Martha is so insecure. If you can think that about her . . . about me.'

'I'm trying to protect her.' So why was I on the defensive?

'From me?' His voice was suddenly charged with emotion. 'Do you seriously imagine I would ever do anything to harm Martha?'

'Not intentionally, no.' I wished I hadn't started this. 'But you have to remember how sensitive Martha is. Her feelings are so easily hurt. I wouldn't want her to—'

'Nor would I. I told you: I'm very fond of Martha. Very, very fond.'

I realized that, for Hugh, this was a passionate declaration of love. I began to relax somewhat.

'I want to marry Martha, death-do-us-part, and live out my lifetime with her. Perhaps even have children of our own . . .'

Everything dissolved into a radiant haze, in the midst of which I sat knitting baby clothes. Then I pulled myself together; I couldn't knit and I wasn't going to bother to learn now. I revised the scenario to swooping through Harrods and Hamley's with open cheque-book. That was more my style.

'Martha is so thoughtful, gentle, kind—' His voice broke. 'I don't want to lose her, Trixie.'

'You won't,' I promised recklessly.

All the same, I was relieved to see that the house was dark when we pulled up in front of it. They hadn't even left a light in the window for me. It was probably just as well.

'Don't get out,' I told Hugh gently. 'They're all asleep. Give me time to talk to Martha in the morning and drop over later.'

CHAPTER 7

I don't know why I bothered to get up for breakfast. The atmosphere at the table was stickier than the redcurrant jam Martha was slathering on her croissant. Evangeline snapped at her toast, producing the sort of crunching sound effects you usually only heard in a horror movie when the monster pounced on its victim and settled down to a light snack—bones and all.

I don't know how she does it; I don't know why she does

it. Well, actually, I do. She only does it to annoy because she knows it teases. That's Evangeline all over.

'Trixie,' Evangeline commanded. 'Please tell Martha I'd like another cup of coffee.'

'*Mother*,' Martha emphasized. 'Please tell *Miss Sinclair* that the coffee-pot is on the stove. One carries the empty cup over to it, lifts the coffee-pot and pours the liquid into the cup—and *that* is how one gets a cup of coffee in *this* kitchen!'

I sighed. It was going to be one of those days. Again. I briefly contemplated going back to bed.

'Considering that *someone* has only recently declared her intention of devoting the rest of her life to us, Trixie, the prospects don't look very bright.'

'*Mother* can have another cup of coffee!' Martha pushed back her chair and dashed for the coffee-pot.

'I haven't finished the first one yet. Watch out!' The boiling liquid slopped over the rim of my cup and into the saucer as Martha poured recklessly.

'Typical!' Evangeline commented to mid-air. She picked up her own cup and saucer and retreated to a fastidious distance as my saucer failed to contain the overflow and a dark brown pool spread across the tablecloth.

'I'm sorry, Mother.' Martha set the coffee-pot down in the butter dish while she grabbed a dish-towel and mopped at the spreading liquid. An oily yellow liquid began seeping from underneath the coffee-pot and added to the dark brown puddle.

Oh well, the tablecloth was ruined anyway. I made a mental note to replace it.

'Darling, don't distress yourself so!' I took the stained and dripping dish-towel (I'd have to replace that, too) and tossed it into the sink.

'Sit down.' I poured Martha a fresh cup of coffee, melted butter dripping from the bottom of the coffee-pot.

'Oh, Mother!' For the first time, Martha noticed what she had done. She stared at the yellow drops, conscience-stricken. 'I'm sorry.'

'Just drink that and relax.' I stripped off the tablecloth, used it to mop up the mess that had seeped through to the wood beneath, wiped off the bottom of the coffee-pot with it, then hurled it into the waste bin. I wasn't even going to try to salvage it.

'I hope that wasn't a family heirloom,' Evangeline said as the lid clanged down.

'Oh, Mother!' Martha burst into tears, horrified at the idea. Of course, that wasn't the only reason for her tears. 'It's all so awful!'

'Everything can be sorted out,' I promised. 'That table-cloth was *not* an heirloom—' I glared at Evangeline—'and we'll replace it. As for ... the rest ...' I approached it delicately. 'I was talking to Hugh last night and he's desperately unhappy about this situation. I do think you ought to talk it over with him.'

'There's nothing more to be said.' For a moment, Martha achieved a precarious dignity, then it broke. 'Oh, Mother!' She was in floods of tears again.

'You see? You're both miserable. There's no point in going on like this. You can work it out. But you've got to meet him face to face and talk to him.'

'I can't! I won't! Oh, Mother!'

'You must. Hugh loves you so much—'

'He does?' She sniffed and brightened.

'You should have heard him!' Now that I had her attention, I embroidered recklessly. 'He loves you passionately, devotedly. He's mad about you!'

'Or just mad,' Evangeline butted in.

'Evangeline,' I said sweetly, through clenched teeth. 'Why don't you go and ... lie down. I'd hate to think we were keeping you from a headache.'

'Don't worry, Mother.' Martha finished wiping her eyes. 'Such remarks are no more than one expects from *Miss Sinclair.*'

'She's better off without him.' Evangeline spoke over Martha's head. 'You can't believe a word that man says. He promised to star us in *Arsenic and Old Lace* and he hasn't done a thing about it.'

'He's looking for a theatre,' I said.

'A likely story!' Evangeline snorted. 'The town is full of theatres. You can't trust a producer. Remember poor Fay Wray? Her producer promised her the tallest, darkest leading man in town—and then he wheeled on *King Kong!*'

'The *right* theatre.' I stuck to the point. 'Hugh feels it's very important that we go into a small intimate theatre where we won't be swamped by too much space.'

'He's looking for a cheap theatre, you mean. We could never be swamped!'

It was nice of her to include me. I was so bowled over, I was momentarily speechless. Martha wasn't.

'Hugh is *not* cheap!'

'Oh no? Just look at your engagement ring!'

'It was his grandmother's.' Martha glanced down at the pearl and garnet ring that had never left her finger, despite the break-up. 'It has great sentimental value.'

'That's what they all say! He couldn't fob off Sir Garrick Erving's daughter with a story like that. *She's* got a rock bigger than Gibraltar—*and* it's a diamond.'

'Really, *Miss Sinclair?* How do *you* know?'

'Evangeline—' If she answered that question, the fat really would be in the fire. 'Stop being so petty! Hugh is doing his best—'

'Unfortunately, as the famous sign in the delicatessen said, "Our best is none too good." He hasn't even had the courtesy to send me a copy of the script yet.'

'If you ask me, you've seen one script too many already.'

'I did not ask you, Trixie. I have no interest in your tatty little opinions.'

'Don't you dare speak to my mother like that! And leave Hugh alone, too. You don't understand one thing about it, *Miss Sinclair!*'

'Evangeline! Martha! Stop it! Both of you!' There was probably something deeply psychological about the way they brought out the childishness in each other.

'*Miss Sinclair* started it!' Martha had shown more sophistication when she was eight years old. Thirty years onward, I could have hoped for better dignity.

'Martha has no sense of humour.' Evangeline sulked, too.

'You're behaving like children! Babies!' Come to think of it, I'd had more patience thirty years ago myself.

'Martha is the childish one,' Evangeline said. 'Next she'll be threatening to run away and join the gipsies. I understand the Council is having trouble with an encampment nearby. In fact, I've seen some of their grubby brats lurking around this morning. I trust you keep the doors locked—we wouldn't want them to get in and steal anything.'

'I always keep the doors locked.' A change of subject was as good as a white flag. I began to breathe more easily.

'It isn't fair to assume that children will be thieves just because they're gipsies.' Martha would fight about anything —so long as she was fighting with Evangeline.

'Never mind that.' I tried to drag them back into the adult world. 'I agree, Evangeline. Hugh *is* taking too long to set up the production. I'll speak to him about it. I'm sure he'll speed things up.' I was certain of it. Now that he knew what feminist film his ex-wife was proposing to make, he could be depended on to do something about it. Getting *Arsenic and Old Lace* into immediate production would remove Evangeline from the film, which would be just as effective as refusing to finance it. Cressida could then blame Evangeline for halting the film and Hugh's access to his children would be unimpaired. It ought to work perfectly. I should have suspected there'd be a catch in it.

'He'd better hurry up.' Evangeline was the catch. 'We're off on location next week.'

'What? When next week? And where?'

'Oh, I don't know.' Evangeline was elaborately casual. 'We'll just get into the taxi on Monday and drive until we see a likely moor.'

'Mm-hmm.' Just what I was afraid of. It was sounding worse by the minute. 'So you go where the spirit moves you. Then what? You sit around waiting for inspiration?'

'You can scoff, Trixie, but those with True Dedication to their Art—'

The telephone rang and she glared at it. I started for it, but she pounced on it first.

'Hello? Hello?' Her eyes narrowed, her nostrils flared. It was *Sorry, Wrong Number* as she would have played it. No wonder Stanwyck got the part. 'Hello?'

After a bit more nostril-flaring, she hung up.

'Who was it?' I asked.

'There was no one there. It must have been for Martha.'

'Mother—'

'With all due respect, the days are gone when your mother could inspire heavy breathers. Frankly, Martha, I didn't think you had it in you, either.'

'Mother—'

'All right, Martha, don't let her upset you. You know that's what she wants.'

'Don't worry, Mother.' Martha was doing her breathing exercises and had regained control. 'Nothing *Miss Sinclair* can say will upset me any longer. As you said, she is just too petty to worry about.'

'That's right. You hang on to that thought.' I turned to Evangeline. 'Before we were so rudely interrupted, you were going to let me see that famous script.'

'Was I? I think not.'

Oh well, it had been worth a try. 'But you're going to, anyway, aren't you? You know I'm dying to see it. And you're dying to show it to me. Come on.'

'You wouldn't appreciate it.' Evangeline loved playing hard-to-get. 'The subtlety of it, the scope, the depth, the—'

'Skip the commercial. Let's see the product!'

'Need you be so crass?' Evangeline moved haughtily to the window and gazed out with the rapt dedicated look of the young widow who had vowed to keep green the memory of her genius husband in *To Tend the Flame*.

'Evangeline, you know perfectly well—'

'What's that?' Evangeline leaned forward suddenly, her eyes sharp and alert. 'What's going on? There's . . . something at the bottom of the garden!' She didn't mean fairies.

'What? Where?' Martha and I both leaped forward to crowd the window with her. Inevitably, the horror at the back of our minds shimmered into vibrant life again. It had all been too recent, too traumatic. Once again we seemed to see the body sprawled on the garden bench, a dark mass with red hair that hadn't been hair at all, but blood.

'It can't be—' The police had taken away the actual garden bench last month for all their forensic tests. But Jasper, for reasons best known to himself, had lost no time in replacing it with a garden swing—despite the oncoming winter. Squinting through the window, I could now discern something large and dark stirring on the swing.

'It's all right, Mother.' Martha's arm was around me reassuringly. 'It's only some neighbourhood children playing on the swing.'

'It's those gipsy brats!' Evangeline rapped on the window-pane sharply. 'Get out! Go away!' She gestured violently at them. 'Scram!'

'They don't mean any harm.' Martha was still on the opposing side. 'A swing is a temptation to any child.'

'Not *our* swing!' Evangeline rapped viciously again. 'They have no right to be here! Go away! Nasty, ugly brats!'

'Take it easy, Evangeline.' I gave her what was intended to be a comforting pat on the arm. We forgot sometimes how much older she really was, and the events of last month had obviously upset her more than she had admitted. 'They're only kids.'

'Brats! Gipsy brats!' She shook off my hand and beat a frantic tattoo on the glass. 'Get them out of here!'

The heap on the swing uncurled itself and turned into two children, looking up at the house with alarm.

'They were asleep,' Martha said. 'You've frightened them.'

'I don't care!' Evangeline realized that she was sliding into the wrong and this only made her more stubborn. 'Everybody knows about gipsies. Give them an inch and they'll take ten miles. Turn a blind eye to the children and you'll have the whole tribe camping out in the garden before you know it.'

The children were exchanging words, their short conversation punctuated by nervous glances towards the kitchen window. Eventually, the young boy took his little sister's hand; they turned and marched bravely towards us, hand in hand, to face the music.

'Don't let them in!' Evangeline turned away from the window abruptly. 'I warn you—I shan't be responsible if you let them take one step inside this house.'

'No one would dream of asking *you* to be responsible for anything, *Miss Sinclair*.' Martha was already on her way to the kitchen door.

I decided I was going to keep out of this. My own opinions were already beginning to form, but I was going to keep them to myself. From this point on, I was just a bystander.

'Hello.' Martha opened the door as they approached. 'Who are you? Do you live near here?'

They stopped a few feet away from the door, staring up at her, wide-eyed.

'Keep them out!' Evangeline ordered. That was all Martha needed.

'Come in.' Martha swung wide the door. 'Come and be friends.'

They advanced a few hesitant steps.

'You're a fool!' Evangeline's voice halted them; it would have halted an army. 'Shut the door, it's freezing here.'

'They look hungry, poor little things,' I murmured. 'I wonder when they last ate.'

'Don't you start!' Evangeline rounded on me. 'And don't give them any cues. They'll only lie about it. Children that age can always eat.'

'Come in,' Martha coaxed. 'Don't pay any attention to *her*.' Her voice hardened. '*Miss Sinclair* doesn't like children.'

'With good reason!' Evangeline glared at her.

The children edged closer to the open door. I wished they'd hurry. Evangeline was right, a freezing wind was sweeping into the room. At this rate, we'd all catch pneumonia.

'That's right,' Martha encouraged. 'Come in here where it's warm. Would you like some toast and jam?'

That did it. They were inside and I breathed a sigh of relief as Martha closed the door. Then I noticed the way they were shivering. I reached out to touch the girl's cheek, but she shrank away as though expecting a blow.

The best thing to do was ignore it. Smiling, I walked over and dropped bread into the toaster. They watched me hungrily.

'You're frozen!' Martha had carried out my original intention and was shocked to the core. Her fingers flinched back from the child's cheek. 'How long have you been out there?'

'All night,' the boy said. 'It's all right,' he added hastily. 'It didn't get really cold until just before daylight.'

'All night!' Martha was appalled. 'Where are your parents? What were they thinking of?'

'We usually sleep in the car,' the boy said. 'But somebody else had to use it last night. They let us into the garden and said they'd come back for us. But I'm afraid they forgot.'

'Forgot! Two children on a winter's night?' For the first time, Martha was realizing that there were more brutal sorts of neglect than the kind she had experienced. 'They should be reported to the police!'

'No, please—' the boy said. The girl began to cry.

I tried to cope with my guilt complex by spooning the hot chocolate powder into mugs. Practical measures would be more appreciated than remorse. Besides, it wasn't my fault that they'd been forgotten.

'*Straight* out of *Father, dear father, come home with me now.*' Evangeline was scornful.

The toast popped up and the plug of the electric kettle snapped out loudly. Both children jumped; they were bundles of nerves. Frozen nerves.

'Here.' I poured the boiling water into their mugs and stirred briskly. 'Come and have your hot chocolate.' They tried to be polite, but they didn't need urging. 'Careful, it's hot.'

'Thank you.' The boy had been taught manners at some point. He nudged his little sister and she gave a fleeting smile, warming her hands on the mug. 'Thank you.'

'Have some milk to cool it down.' I splashed some into their mugs while Martha buttered the toast and put more slices in the toaster.

'Ridiculous!' Evangeline snorted. 'All this fuss over a couple of gipsy brats. Who are they?'

'I'm Orl—Orrie.' The boy introduced himself politely. 'And this is my sister . . . Vi.'

'Ridiculous!' Evangeline said again. 'What frightful names!'

'Yes.' Unexpectedly, the boy agreed with her. 'We have —had—nicer names once. But Mummy—Mum—says we mustn't use them any more. Because they're elitist.'

'Evangeline,' I said quickly, before anyone could grasp that this wasn't quite gipsy talk. 'Why don't you go and find a couple of sweaters for the kids to wear? They've got a lot of thawing out to do.'

'Oh, very well!' Evangeline's martyred sigh did not quite mask the fact that she was unnerved. The boy had a clear, carrying voice; the sort that would bounce off the back wall of the upper balcony with very little training. Blood will out.

'Put plenty of jam on it.' Ministering to the children, Martha hadn't noticed. 'There's lots more.' She left the plate of toast in front of them and moved back to confer with me.

'This is terrible, Mother. What are we to do? We've got to notify somebody. The police? The National Society for the Prevention of Cruelty to Children? The Social Services?'

'Let's not be too hasty.' I had to keep her from doing anything like that. Hugh wouldn't appreciate it. Cressida might be a lousy mother, but he wouldn't want the fact blazoned all over the newspapers. There are certain kinds of publicity you can do without. Across the years, Evangeline and I have become experts in most of them.

'What do you suggest then? We can't just—just—'

'There's plenty of time,' I said soothingly. 'No one seems to be looking for them.'

'That's terrible! I thought even gipsies had more feeling for their children. How can any mother be so unnatural?'

'Here you are.' Unfortunately, Evangeline made her entrance right on cue. She glared at Martha and handed two cardigans to me.

'Cashmere?' I couldn't believe her generosity. I was right.

'They're Martha's,' she said. 'I knew she wouldn't mind. She's the one fawning over the brats.'

'Evangeline—'

'*Miss Sinclair* is right, Mother. I don't mind. In fact, I'd have suggested it if I'd been thinking fast enough.' Martha took one cardigan from me and wrapped it around Vi, while I took care of Orrie.

'Thank you.' This time, Vi didn't need prompting. She rubbed her fingertips clean on her jeans and then stroked the cashmere luxuriously. 'Oooh, it's lovely.'

Orrie wriggled his neck against the softness before he said, in the tone of one who had learned a bitter lesson. 'Cashmere is elitist, too.'

'*We* are elitist,' Evangeline said majestically. 'And we've damned well earned the right to be.'

Vi broke into a little grin; she exchanged glances with her brother. It was obviously a new idea to the children—and not an unwelcome one.

'How old are you?' I asked.

'I'm nine and Vi's seven.'

'Shouldn't you be in school?' Evangeline inquired severely.

'It might be school holidays,' I suggested. 'They're different here.'

'Actually, we're changing schools at the moment,' Orrie said. 'Mum decided the boarding-schools we were in were—'

'Don't tell me, let me guess,' I interrupted. 'Too elitist!'

They nodded solemnly, uneasily. They were not accustomed to having fun poked at their mother's views.

'We're sorry to be such a bother,' Orrie apologized. 'I'm sure they'll remember where we are and come to collect us soon.'

'Have some more toast.' Martha set another plateful of toast down in front of them and retreated back to me. 'We

can't let them go,' she whispered. 'Who knows what will
happen to them? I'm going to call the police.'

'Later.' I caught her arm as she tried to dash away. 'First,
I think a nice hot bath is indicated as soon as they've
finished breakfast. Then we'll put them to bed with hot
water bottles and aspirin. *Then* we can sit down and decide
what we'll do about the situation.' I was thankful to see that
the first dreadful shivering had stopped. 'Those children will
be lucky if they haven't caught a nasty cold.'

'Yes. Yes, you're right,' Martha said. A hot bath must be
next on the agenda for them. Poor little—'

The sharp peal of the doorbell cut her off.

'That will be Mum now,' Orrie said confidently.

CHAPTER 8

'Goot morning, Trreexie.' Griselda von Kirstenberg
brushed past me. 'I wish to see Evangeline.'

'I'm not sure she's in.' I was pretty sure she didn't want
to see Griselda.

'No, no, Treexie. I must see her. I know she is here.'

'How do you—?' A sudden thought struck me. 'Did you
telephone us here a little while ago?'

'Of course. Und that is how I know you are at home.'
With a smug smile, she swept into the living-room and
draped herself on a corner of the crimson velvet sofa. Personally, I wouldn't have been so smug if I knew the only way
somebody would be at home to me was if I'd tricked them
into admitting it.

'Und now you will let Evangeline know that I am here
and must speak to her.'

'She may have a headache . . .' It looked like her last
resort.

'I have aspirins in my bag.'

'Well, bully for you!' Evangeline *would* be pleased. I couldn't wait to see her face. On second thoughts, I'd rather wait—indefinitely.

The doorbell rang again, postponing the evil moment.

'Excuse me.' I dashed thankfully to answer it. Although, if it turned out to be Cressida returning for her neglected children, there would be a nasty scene of a different sort—starring Martha.

'Good morning, Trixie.' Detective-Sergeant Singer beamed down at me. 'It's all right. Evangeline is expecting me. We're going to make a start on her autobiography this morning.' He flourished a bouquet of roses at me as though they were some additional password.

'Oh, what a beautiful morning,' I murmured. 'Go straight through. The queue is forming in the living-room. I'll send Evangeline in to you.'

'Splendid! Splendid!' He obviously thought it was. With jaunty step, he proceeded into the living-room and I heard his joyous cry: 'No! It's Griselda von Kirstenberg, isn't it?'

I hurried back to the kitchen. Evangeline was not going to be pleased at the prospect of sharing her fan's attention. That's the trouble with film buffs, they tend to be indiscriminate. Any old star will do. The older, the better—and he was hitting the jackpot with Griselda.

'Evangeline—' She was already in the hallway; she was expecting Sergeant Singer. She wasn't expecting Griselda.

'Yes,' I know,' she said. 'He's late.'

'He's not alone—' I tried to warn her.

'He's brought a photographer?' She preened. 'How naughty! He wasn't supposed to do the photographs until later. I suppose the dear boy couldn't wait.'

'It's not exactly a photographer—'

But she had already reached the doorway and discovered

that for herself. She backed out faster than she had started in.

'What's that woman doing here?' she demanded of me. 'Is she taking up residence?'

'Be fair,' I said. 'It's only the second time she's been here.'

'In as many days!' Evangeline was working herself into a towering fury. 'Why did you let her know I was in?'

'She already knew. You answered the telephone to her. She was the nobody that was there.'

'She tricked us!'

'She sure did!' We faced each other grimly, and suddenly we were back in the 'Tomboy's Revenge' flashback of *Under the Weeping Willow*. I could almost feel the sunbonnet strings tighten under my chin; Evangeline tugged at her skirt, as she had always tugged at the gingham pinafore just before the shooting started. In my mind's eye, the great dark set loomed over us again, the furniture built to an impossible scale to dwarf us to pre-teen size.

I spat on the palm of my hand. Evangeline spat on the palm of her hand. We slapped hands together, swearing revenge on the High School sneak who had betrayed our confidences.

'No grass will ever grow again!' I intoned.

'Never again!' Evangeline vowed.

Hand in hand, we wheeled to face the grown-up enemies who were about to come through the doorway.

'My God!' Sergeant Singer stood there. 'That was the scene from *Under the Weeping Willow*. You can still do it. For a moment, I'd have sworn you were both ten years old.'

'It's called acting, dear,' Evangeline informed him.

'Or second childhood.' Griselda was in the doorway behind him. 'You appeared—you disappeared. We came to see if anything is wrong. And we find you here—playing!'

'It was great! Marvellous! A memory to treasure!' Singer couldn't believe his luck. He hadn't been able to believe it since he followed his boss into a murder investigation and found that the major suspects had all been major Hollywood Stars of the Golden Age.

'This is wasting time,' Griselda decided. She spread herself all over the doorway again, just to show what *she* could do.

'*The Lady from Limbo*,' he gasped in delight. 'Also *The Baroness Bows Out* and *Stormclouds on the Rhine*, and—'

'Etcetera, etcetera.' Evangeline cut him off before he could recite every one of Griselda's credits. She had played that scene in every picture she had ever appeared in. The hot betting among the technical crews had been that she didn't know any other way to enter a room. Her fellow stars had often suggested kicking her across the threshold. There would have been no shortage of volunteers.

'Er . . .' Belatedly, the atmosphere seemed to be getting to Sergeant Singer. It was just as well his job called for him to deduce and not intuit. '*Is* everything all right?'

'What could possibly be wrong?' Evangeline gave him an enchanting smile.

'There *is* something wrong.' He was getting the message, but didn't quite know what to do with it.

'We have been having such an interesting chat.' Not even Western Union could get through to Griselda. 'You did not tell me you had such a charming young man . . . in attendance. We must have a long talk.'

'Ulp!' Sgt Singer swallowed audibly and a dark crimson tide surged up to engulf his face. 'No—No—' he blurted. 'You misunderstand. I'm just helping Miss Sinclair with her autobiography. We're writing it together.'

'So? You have a handsome young collaborator. I had not thought of having someone to help me write *my* memoirs—' She turned rapacious eyes on Singer. 'Until now.'

'If you need any help—' Despite his nervousness, a certain rapaciousness of his own gleamed in Singer's eyes. Obviously, he could see himself cornering the market in ancient glamour girls. 'I'm sure I'd have enough time to—'

'Oh? Have you resigned from the police force, then?' Evangeline inquired coldly. 'I shouldn't think your official duties left you with all that much free time.'

'They don't—usually. But we're in a quiet patch right now. And I have some leave due. Overdue.'

'How convenient for you. I trust you will use it . . . *wisely*.' Evangeline bared her teeth in a way that left him in no doubt as to her meaning.

'Oh, certainly, certainly,' he said quickly. 'We're already started on your book. That will take priority. I just thought . . . later . . . when you're working . . .'

'Working?' Griselda could not keep the jealousy out of her voice. 'What are you doing?'

'Hugh's mounting a special production for us,' I said, before Evangeline had a chance to say anything about *King Lear*—or rather, *Queen Leah*. The longer we could keep that little turkey under wraps, the easier it would be to wring its neck before it got loose on an unsuspecting world. 'As soon as he can find a suitable theatre, we'll start rehearsals. We're doing a revival of *Arsenic and Old Lace*.'

'How sweet,' Griselda purred. 'They are still typecasting. Evangeline, of course, will play Arsenic.'

Singer turned the laugh into a cough just in time. Evangeline's narrowed eyes were throwing off deadly sparks. But, if looks could kill, Griselda would never have lasted this long.

'Mother . . .'

'Excuse me.' I had never been more delighted to hear Martha bleating for me. 'I must go and see what my daughter wants.'

*

It was a problem I could deal with. Martha had suddenly
panicked at the thought of giving baths to two small children. Together, we managed quite nicely. Orrie, in fact,
indignantly refused all help, but little Vi seemed to revel in
having so much attention. Their heads had scarcely touched
the pillows before they were asleep. I tucked hot-water
bottles up against their feet and pulled the covers up under
their chins. Martha drew the curtains to darken the room
and tiptoed to the door. She needn't have bothered—those
kids were out for the count. They wouldn't surface again
for hours.

'Mother, what are we to do about them?' She began again
as soon as we closed the door behind us.

'Let's do nothing,' I said craftily. 'I've been thinking it
over and I think we should just take care of them for a few
days and keep quiet about it. Let's see how long it takes
their precious Mum to miss them—and let her worry about
them for a while. It sounds as though it would make quite
a change for her.'

'You're right! People like that don't deserve to have
children. If they can't take better care of them, they should
put them up for adoption. They're a disgrace to the human
race!'

'It *was* pretty appalling to leave those children out in the
garden all night.' Martha was fomenting nicely. 'Of course,
she might not have remembered where she left them.'

'Even worse! To think of no knowing where your children
are at night! Even *Miss Sinclair* wasn't that bad!'

'Evangeline did her best for you—by her lights.' This
was the closest we had ever come to a discussion of it. 'I
tried, too.'

'You were wonderful, Mother!' Unexpectedly, she turned
and embraced me. 'I always appreciated it. You're my *real*,
true mother. But . . . I . . . I just can't talk about it yet.'

'That's all right, my darling.' I returned her embrace.

'You're my *real, true* daughter. We both know that. Nothing —and nobody—else matters.' I controlled a sentimental sniffle; Martha would never forgive me if I began blubbing at this late stage.

'Now,' I said briskly, 'we're agreed, aren't we? The kids are *our* little secret.'

'Yes, yes.' Martha was now downright enthusiastic about the idea. In a very short time she would be convinced that she had thought of it herself. 'But . . . what about Miss Sinclair? Won't she give the game away?'

'Leave Evangeline to me,' I said rashly.

Evangeline, as I had thought, had problems of her own.

'Did you hear that woman?' she demanded, when I ventured into the hallway after waiting a suitable interval after the slam of the front door. 'Did you *see* the shameless hussy? Did you *hear* her?'

'Mm-hmm. Trying to steal your thunder, wasn't she?'

'Worse! She was trying to steal my ghost. And right in front of me! As though I was . . . negligible!'

'Never!' I shook my head. Whatever else Evangeline was, she could never be considered negligible.

'The nerve of her!' Evangeline tossed her head.

'Why are you worrying?' I tried to drag her back to practicalities. 'She's been threatening those memoirs for decades and hasn't produced them yet. You know we decided she just used the threat as a form of genteel blackmail. She'll never get down to writing anything—that would destroy her source of income.'

'I'm not so sure. Remember that a lot of her sources have been dying off over the years. In the natural course of things, the rest of them will die eventually. And those who are left behind won't have the same vested interest in preserving the dear departed's reputation. Quite the contrary, some of them are breaking their necks to cash in on past scandals.

Look at all those exposés the children of the stars are publishing now.'

'There seems to be an insatiable market for it,' I agreed. 'I suppose it's all the Late-Late TV showings and the museum programmes. We used to be entertainment; now we're Popular Culture.'

'The audience may not be quite so large these days, but they're more intense—'

There was a moment's pause as we involuntarily reflected on what that intensity had meant for one person.

'We have acquired cult status,' Evangeline went on briskly. 'There are a lot of people out there who want to know what *really* happened. Grisly could make a lot of money if she wrote a no-holds-barred memoir. And, with someone to do the actual writing for her, she might get down to it.'

'Griselda was having dinner with Job Farraday at the Harpo last night.' Something stirred at the back of my mind again at the mention of long-ago scandals and mysteries.

'Job Farraday?' Evangeline's eyes widened. 'Is *he* still around? I haven't thought about him in years.'

'He's been working over here ever since he left Hollywood. He left under some kind of cloud, didn't he? Not just that nonsense about being a suspected Communist.'

'Job would never have gone in for Communism,' Evangeline said firmly. 'He never believed in sharing *anything*. But yes, there *was* something hushed-up . . . something about one of his films . . .' She frowned, trying to remember. 'Or . . . more than one . . .'

'*Very* hushed-up,' I prompted. 'I can't quite recall what it was all about.'

'It was before your time—in Hollywood.' That was an admission Evangeline seldom made. She hated to remember that I was younger. 'There were two . . . incidents . . . accidents . . . involving several people . . .' She had a far-away look. 'The first was away back. The second was just before he left Hollywood. Both happened on pictures he was directing . . .'

'Accidents . . .' It was coming back to me: the whispers, nods, winks, hints. Nothing too obvious, but something nasty bubbling beneath the surface. On the surface, Hollywood was protecting its own—especially when they were big money-makers. 'Fatal accidents . . .'

'Stunts that went wrong,' Evangeline said distantly. 'Because of cutting corners . . . holding down expenses . . . forcing stuntmen to work too fast . . . safety equipment not good enough . . .'

'And a few more Indians bit the dust!'

'A stuntman, actually, and a couple of extras . . . the first time.'

'I suppose the accident rate isn't really any higher than it is in other industries.' I tried to be fair. 'It's just that when something goes wrong in film-making, it gets a lot more publicity.'

'Especially when something *keeps* going wrong. To have one accident is unfortunate—' Evangeline arched her eyebrows, pitched her voice higher and became Lady Bracknell. 'To have a *series* of accidents—'

'Is to get a reputation for being a jinx.' I was right there with her. Apart from the fatal accidents, there had been several minor—but disabling to those concerned—accidents. There was more than one reason why Job Farraday had left Hollywood. 'Still, he seems to have done all right over here. Maybe he left his jinx behind him.'

'Or perhaps we just haven't heard about it, if he's had any further trouble on this side. He'd scarcely issue a Press Release about it.'

'Press Release?' Sergeant Singer stood in the doorway of the living-room. 'Am I missing something? A Press Release about your autobiography?'

'Oh, I thought you'd gone,' I said. Evangeline had been in no hurry to get back to him.

'No, that was Griselda,' he said. 'She had another appointment. She asked me to tell you that she'd see you later.'

'Not if I see her first!' Evangeline snarled.

Singer started to laugh, then wisely thought better of it. 'Er, are we ready to start now?'

'Start?' She was making clear that he had lost favour.

'Reminiscing. Er, writing your book.'

'If you're sure you're still interested in *me*.' Evangeline wasn't going to let him off the hook easily.

'Oh yes! Yes!' He was suddenly panic-stricken at the thought of losing her. 'You were the most fascinating woman in Hollywood. Your public is longing to read your story.'

'Well . . .' Evangeline thawed only slightly. She wasn't too pleased by that *were*.

'Oh, go ahead,' I said. 'You can use Jasper's study upstairs.' I knew that had already been arranged with Jasper, he was spending most of his time with a new girl-friend these days and had no use for it himself. 'It's at the back of the house and nice and quiet, so you won't be disturbed,' I added for Sergeant Singer's benefit, in case he had forgotten the topography of the house.

'Fine!' he said with bogus heartiness. It struck me that he had lost something of his enthusiasm for being shut up alone with Evangeline. And he hadn't seen her in her worst mood yet.

While Evangeline was still hesitating, the doorbell rang. That decided her.

'Come along, Singer,' Evangeline ordered sharply, start-ing up the staircase. She wasn't going to risk Griselda's having had second thoughts and returning unexpectedly. 'Trixie can deal with whoever it is.'

Singer trailed her up the stairs slowly and I waited until

he was out of sight. It was only fair. Evangeline had seen him first. Let Griselda find her own ghost.

The doorbell rang again and I went to answer it.

CHAPTER 9

Nova stood on the doorstep, looking both apologetic and nerve-racked. 'Sorry to trouble you—' she began.

'No trouble at all.' I took a swift glance over my shoulder at the deserted hallway behind me and settled down to brazen it out. 'Do come in.'

'I can't stay.' She shuffled in uneasily and looked around. 'You got home all right then, last night?'

'Of course. Hugh delivered me right to the door.'

'Actually,' she confessed, 'I know you did. I sort of hung around to make sure you were all right.'

'Whatever for?' So that *was* where she had been while the kids had been shivering in the cold. 'I told you I'd be taken care of.'

'I wasn't so sure of that. I knew you were running to meet Hugh—and you can't trust *him*. Look at the way he's treated poor Cres.'

'I don't really know her—' And the more I heard of her, the less I wanted to. 'But I thought he was treating her rather well. He's financing her new production, isn't he?'

'Oh, uh, yes . . .' She hadn't known I knew that. 'I mean, psychologically. Look at the way he's ready to let them re-release that terrible old series portraying her as a sex object and a bimbo.'

'She *did* make the series in the first place. No one forced her to take that role.'

'Maybe not physically,' Nova said darkly. 'But there were other pressures in those days. And it was before her consciousness was raised. Now she realizes how exploited she was—that they were using her body and denying her brains—'

'Mmm-hmm.' I wouldn't like to take any bets on those brains. It sounded to me as though she had just swapped one set of clichés for another.

'Oh, we appreciate Hugh's financial support,' Nova assured me anxiously, perhaps fearing I might report back to him. 'Even though it's the least he can do. I mean, Cres hopes it means that *his* consciousness is being raised and that one day—' She broke off in confusion.

So Cressida was hoping for an eventual reconciliation with Hugh, was she? Or just with his bankroll? Either way, it boded ill for my poor Martha.

'Anyway—' Nova hurried to change the subject—'that's beside the point. What I really came here to ask you is—' She broke off again, obviously finding it difficult to word her question.

'Yes?'

'Have you . . . have you seen a couple of children wandering around here?'

'*Chil-dren?*' I did the Lady Bracknell bit myself. 'What *sort* of . . . *chil-dren?*' I let my voice soar into the upper levels of incredulity.

'Oh, well,' Nova muttered. 'It was just an off-chance. I didn't really suppose they'd have stuck around. They probably wandered off home.' She looked worried—and rightly. For the length of time those children had been abandoned, they'd had enough time to hike all around London and back.

'Wandering? At night? Around here?' I let Lady Bracknell's disapproval wash over her. She deserved to worry. 'I don't like the sound of that. We aren't very far from the Grand Union Canal, you know.'

'Oh my God!' She hadn't known. She went so pale that

I almost felt sorry for her. Then I remembered those two abandoned waifs shivering through the long dark night and hardened my heart.

'Look—' She stumbled towards the door. 'I've got to go. They can't have—' She was wrenching desperately at the doorknob. 'Orrie's careful. They couldn't possibly—' She was trying to convince herself, not me.

'Here.' I slipped the latch for her. 'Are you sure you can't stay for a cup of tea? What's this all about? What children —?' If only the cameras had been trained on me, I'd have been a cinch for an Oscar.

'Later.' She tore open the door and plunged down the steps. 'I'll explain later—'

She leaped into the taxi and sped off while I was still standing in the doorway registering amazement and concern.

She shot out of the drive without even pausing to check that the road was clear. I saw an unwary pedestrian dodge back just in time.

My conscience gave me a sharp jab. If Nova hit anyone in her desperate dash to the Canal, it would be my fault. I should have told her the children were here and safe . . .

I became aware of a delicious fragrance wafting through the hallway behind me. Martha was making her allspice drop cookies for tea. The children were in for a treat.

I cheered up immediately, taking it as a sign that I had been right, after all. The longer Martha and the children had to get to know each other, the better.

I stepped back and was about to close the door when the pedestrian reappeared and began marching purposefully up the drive. His face was hidden behind a big bouquet of flowers and he was balancing a couple of oddly-shaped parcels. I had just decided he was a rather inexpert delivery man when he began waving one of the parcels at me.

'Miss Dolan—' he yodelled. 'Miss Dolan—don't shut the door. It's me! Trevor!'

'Trevor?' I managed to place him just before it became embarrassing: the waiter from the Harpo. 'Trevor, what are you doing here?'

'I have come—' he staggered up the steps—'to throw myself on your mercy. Here—' He thrust the bouquet at me. 'This is for you.'

'How sweet of you. But you shouldn't have—' I was pretty sure his income didn't run to such gestures. On the other hand, Hugh had tipped quite lavishly last night.

'Oh yes I should. You don't know what I want yet. I know I've got a terrible nerve, but I couldn't think of anyone else. Please, please, help me—it's my big chance!'

'Come in.' I didn't know what he had in mind, but we couldn't resolve anything standing on the doorstep.

'Oh, thank you!' He tilted a long flat parcel to get it through the doorway. I was glad he'd already given me the flowers, otherwise I'd have suspected he'd found the longest-stemmed roses in existence. His other parcel was smaller and chunkier. Frankly, I didn't like the look of either of them.

'Now—' I led him into the living-room and perched on the edge of a chair, regarding him warily as he sat on the sofa and clutched his parcels to him. 'What's your problem?'

'Oh, Miss Dolan, I don't know how to tell you—' He took a deep breath and I knew he'd been practising for hours. 'It's too awful of me! I wouldn't blame you if you never spoke to me again, but—'

'But—?' I prompted.

'It was too awful of me,' he began again. 'But I couldn't help overhearing what you were saying to Mr Carpenter last night. About your daughter. About her being an archery expert—'

'Archery . . .' I echoed. Suddenly, the enormously long

flat parcel and the shorter stubbier one were no longer so mysterious.

'Miss Dolan—' His anxious eyes pleaded with me. 'Miss Dolan, when I told Mr Farraday last night that *I* could handle a bow and arrow, I—' He lowered his gaze and bowed his head. 'I *lied*!'

'No!' I tried to sound surprised.

'Yes,' he confessed. 'I never went near a bow and arrow in my whole life. It was all a lie when I said I had to go home and collect my equipment. But—' he brightened— 'it got me the audition. Monday afternoon. So I rushed out first thing this morning and bought a bow and arrows from a sports shop. Only . . . only it isn't as easy as it looks. And the sports shop didn't give instructions. They gave me the names of a couple of archery clubs where I could get lessons. But not without an appointment. And not immediately,' he concluded with a passionate wail. 'It's the weekend!'

I knew just what he meant. The English weekend, at its worst, can last from Thursday to Tuesday; at its best, it was Saturday afternoon through Sunday night. There were several permutations in between but, whichever way you counted it, Sunday was a dead day. And tomorrow was a Sunday.

'Oh, please, Miss Dolan. If you'd just speak to her. Ask her to see me. All I need is a few essentials and I can fake it from there well enough for the audition. I'll pay anything—'

'Martha wouldn't want money.' I was sure of that. 'If she did it, it would be as a personal favour.'

'I'd be so grateful—'

'Let's go and see her.'

'Well, I don't know . . .' Martha was trying to pretend that she wasn't flattered and deeply gratified. 'I haven't touched a bow in years . . .'

'But you don't forget, do you?' Trevor asked anxiously. 'It comes back—like swimming and riding a bicycle.'

'Surely you can manage it, darling.'

'I've brought everything along.' Trevor began tearing the wrappings off his parcels. 'The bow . . . the arrows . . .'

'The target?' Martha inquired gently.

'Target?' His face fell. 'Don't we just aim at a tree or something? No, no, I can see that might ruin the trees. I . . . I hadn't thought about a target. The salesman didn't mention it.'

'What about that terrible sofa cushion?' I had a bright idea. 'The one that was so hard and uncomfortable we hid it away in the box-room?'

'Yes,' Martha conceded, 'that might do. Just to start with. And it's so awful that no one would mind if we destroyed it.'

'They'd give us a vote of thanks,' I said firmly. 'It should have been thrown out years ago—if only Beau weren't so cheap. I'll go and get it.'

When I returned with the cushion, Martha and Trevor were out in the back yard, already engrossed in the first lesson.

Following Martha's instructions, I propped the cushion up against a bush at the far end of the garden and stepped out of the way.

Martha casually let the first arrow fly and it thudded into the cushion, just slightly to the left of the heart of a nasty hibiscus in the centre of the chintz cover.

'Wonderful!' Trevor applauded. 'Oh, Miss Dolan, if you can only teach me to shoot like that, I'll be your slave for life!'

'Call me Martha.' Trevor had just won her heart. After a lifetime of watching ardent fans cluster around me and Evangeline, Martha was enchanted at the notion of collecting a few fans of her own. Another arrow hummed past me and landed beside the first one.

'Fantastic!' Trevor was a great audience. 'Brilliant! Martha, you're a genius!'

'Here—' Smiling, Martha handed over the bow. 'Now you try it. Er, Mother, you'd better come up here with us.'

That wasn't a bad idea. Trevor thoughtfully waited until I was beside them before he loosed his arrow. It flew wide of the mark and disappeared into the undergrowth at just about the spot where I had been standing.

'Oh, Miss Dolan!' He gasped in horror. 'I might have killed you!'

'Call me Trixie,' I said. 'And don't worry. That's why Martha called me up here. She isn't going to let you make any silly mistakes like that.'

'I'm certainly not!' Martha fitted another arrow into place and demonstrated again. Trevor watched attentively.

I glanced upwards and saw a face at the window of Jason's study. Sergeant Singer was looking down on us, rather wistfully, I thought. Then he turned away, obviously recalled to duty by Evangeline. That reminded me. There was something else I wanted to do while the coast was clear.

'I'll leave you two to get on with it,' I told Martha and went back into the house.

I stood in the hallway, listening. No sound from Martha's room; the children were still sleeping peacefully. Only the gentlest murmur of sound from outside, as Martha continued her tuition. No creak of the stairs suggested that anyone was descending. If Evangeline was well launched into a monologue of her early life and experiences, she was good for a couple more hours yet.

The coast was clear.

I slipped into Evangeline's room and began searching. It wasn't under her pillow; I hadn't expected it to be. Pillows were for leaving love-letters under or notes of farewell pinned to the top of; every actress worth her salt knew that. It wasn't in the closet (for bodies to fall out of, or lovers to hide in when a raging husband bursts into the room). Nor was it beneath the lingerie in the bureau drawers (that was for letters again—either of love or blackmail, sometimes both).

The Purloined Letter! I found it second from the top in a stack of magazines and carried it back to my room where I stretched out on the chaise-longue with the script and a paperback copy of *King Lear* I had acquired earlier. I had the strong suspicion that it was going to be better to take this lying down.

How right I was. Half an hour later the script slid from my nerveless fingers. I closed my eyes and concentrated on slow deep breathing; it would do no good at all to have hysterics.

A sudden cheering thought occurred to me: perhaps I was already hysterical. Perhaps I was hallucinating. I opened the paperback and read again Lear's raging exit speech, Act II, Scene iv:

> '. . . *No, you unnatural hags,*
> *I will have such revenges on you both,*
> *That all the world shall—I will do such things—*
> *What they are, yet I know not; but they shall be*
> *The terrors of the earth. You think I'll weep;*
> *No, I'll not weep:*
> *I have full cause of weeping; but this heart*
> *Shall break into a hundred thousand flaws,*
> *Or ere I'll weep.—O fool, I shall go mad!*'

With which, Lear exits, as well he might, accompanied by Gloucester, Kent and his Fool. The stage directions then called for *Storm and Tempest.* That was clear enough—and all good powerful stuff.

I took one more deep breath and retrieved the *Queen Leah* script from the floor. I flipped to the rough equivalent of Act II, Scene iv, and took another look at the misbegotten Lucy's transliteration. Very rough, indeed:

> *'No, no, no! You lousy poofter pricks!*
> *I'll get you for this—both of you!*
> *Don't ask me how or when, but I'll get you—'*

Absently, I stuffed a paper handkerchief into my mouth to keep from screaming and continued to read. I tried to imagine Evangeline delivering those lines, but they kept coming out in Jimmy Cagney's voice. I had already noticed that Lucy was not strong on spelling and it was becoming more apparent. She couldn't even spell the words right when they had only four letters in them. I continued grimly to the wind-up:

> *'You're not going to make me cry—*
> *Maybe I'll crack up, but*
> *Before I cry, I'll go crazy!*
> *You see what you're doing?*
> *You're driving me crazy!*
> *Crazy! Do you hear me? Crazy!'*

My fingers twitched away from it and the script slid back to the floor—where it belonged. Someone was crazy around here—and that someone was Evangeline. How could she take a shambles like that seriously? No wonder she'd tried to keep me from seeing it.

The telephone rang abruptly. I broke the record for the sitting broadjump and snatched up the receiver before the second ring. I didn't want anyone coming to investigate before I had a chance to get that incriminating evidence back into the pile of magazines in Evangeline's room.

'Mmm-ph?'

'Hello? Trixie? Trixie, is that you?'

'Mm-ph! Ulph!' I spat out wads of soggy tissue. 'Yes. Hello, Hugh. Rotten line, isn't it. Although it seems better now.'

'Yes. Yes, I can hear you now.'

'And I can hear you. Yes, it's *much* better.' I chased a few more soggy pellets around my gumline with my tongue.

'Are you all right, Trixie? You sound . . . rather odd.'

'To tell the truth—' I discovered it *was* the truth—'I've got a terrible headache.'

'I'm sorry. Are you doing anything for it?'

'Only a bonfire could cure me.'

'What?'

'This connection isn't perfect yet,' I said hastily. 'You sound quite strange yourself, Hugh.'

He sighed deeply. It was most unlike him.

'Hugh?' I was suddenly alarmed. 'Hugh, is anything wrong?'

'That's what I was calling about, Trixie. I . . . I'm terribly sorry, but I'm afraid I won't be able to get over there after all, this afternoon.' It was that old English understatement, in Voice of Doom tones.

'Hugh, what is it? What's wrong? Is there anything I can do?'

'Do?' He gave a hollow laugh—I think it was supposed to be a laugh. It could also have passed for a sob. 'Thank you, Trixie, that's very kind of you. But there's nothing you can do.' That strange sound came again. 'There may be nothing *any* of us can do.'

'Hugh, tell me!' He was obviously dying to. 'You can't come here—shall I go over there?'

'No, no,' he said quickly. 'I'm not at home. I'm sorry, Trixie, I'd love to have you here for moral support. But I can't—can't—' He broke off, choking.

'Hugh, for God's sake—what is it?'

'The children . . .' he said brokenly. 'The children . . . are missing. Cressida is afraid they've . . . been kidnapped.'

'Kidnapped? That's ridiculous!' But I could see Cressida's point. If the children had subsequently been found floating in the Grand Union Canal, she and her friends would be absolved of all blame. It would have been the 'kidnappers' panicking for some unknown reason and disposing of captives old enough to identify them and testify against them.

'Why should it be so ridiculous?' Hugh was getting stuffy. 'We haven't had much chance to get to know much about each other, but I can assure you that I am a person of some substance. I am also, unfortunately, in the public eye from time to time as my shows become hits. As Cressida pointed out . . . I should have taken precautions a long time ago. I should have arranged bodyguards for the children. And now . . .' He choked again. 'Now . . . it's too late.'

'Hugh, listen to me—' I was developing a strong dislike for his ex-wife. I was also beginning to realize why Martha held such an attraction for him. My sweet innocent darling might have her faults, but never in a thousand years could she have thought up such an evil scenario. Hugh might not have been able to put into words the difference between her and Cressida, but he sensed it.

'Trixie, there's nothing you can say. I'm sorry, I'll get back to you as soon as I can. But you must understand, I have to leave the line clear, in case . . . in case the kidnappers are trying to reach us with the ransom demand.'

'Hugh, take a deep breath and listen to me. Don't say anything—just listen. The children are here.'

CHAPTER 10

There was such a long silence I wondered if he'd fainted.

'Hugh? Did you hear me? The children are here. They're safe and well. That is—' I was caught by sudden doubt— 'they *are* Orrie and Vi, aren't they?'

'Orrie and Vi?' It sounded like a faint echo on the other end of the line.

'Because Orlando and Viola were too elitist. A little girl with long golden curls—well, she would have long golden curls, if some idiot hadn't given her a crew cut—and a boy with a fantastic voice?'

'Yes . . . Yes . . .' he said slowly, still trying to take it in. 'But . . . I don't understand. How did you find them? How did you get them away from the kidnappers?'

'Hugh—' I tried to talk him out of his state of shock. 'There *were* no kidnappers. The children are here. Martha has them—'

'Martha?' The name snapped him back to reality. 'What's Martha doing with them?'

'Martha found them at the bottom of the garden this morning. She's fed them, given them a hot bath—and now they're fast asleep in Martha's bed.'

'In Martha's bed,' he echoed wistfully. 'But—' His voice became firmer, he was beginning to assimilate the information. 'But what were they doing in your garden this morning? Cressida said they'd been missing since yesterday afternoon. She's only just got up enough courage to tell me.'

'I'm sorry, Hugh.' Now it was my turn to apologize. 'I'm afraid that it was my fault—in a roundabout way. I didn't know—I had no idea—or it never would have happened. But it seems that Nova turned them out of the taxi so that she could drive me to the Harpo. Then she didn't trust you to see me home safely, so she hung around until we came out after dinner and she saw that I was all right. Then she went to look for the children and they weren't where she had left them.'

'Left them . . .' The echo was back on the line.

'Meanwhile, the children had grown bored and weren't really sure whether or not she was coming back. They wandered around—and discovered the swing at the bottom of the garden. Hugh—?' The silence was alarming me.

'Hugh, it's all right. It was quite a mild night. And there was a car rug on the hammock. They're all right. With luck, they may not even have caught a cold.'

'*My* children—' Hugh's voice was tight and cold, with a hard note in it I had never heard before. '*My* children—sleeping rough!'

'Hugh—'

'Thank you, Trixie. I'll be right over. And thank Martha, too. In fact, could you let me speak to Martha? Just for a moment?'

'It might not be a good idea just yet. She doesn't know they're *your* children. She thinks they came from the gipsy encampment we've got in the neighbourhood. They were cold and hungry and frightened—that was all that mattered to Martha. She's taken them under her wing—and they like it there. Give them more time to get to know each other. Believe me, Hugh, it might work.'

'You may be right, Trixie, but I'd still like a word with Martha. If you could get her to the phone . . .'

'She's awfully busy right now . . .' We both knew that my chances of getting her to speak to him were still slim, but I tried to soften the blow. 'You remember that sweet little waiter last night?' It already seemed a century ago. 'The one who said he was an archery expert? Well, he didn't really know a thing about it, but he heard me telling you about Martha. He showed up here this afternoon and threw himself on her mercy. She's out in the garden with him now, giving him lessons.'

'Martha—' I was happy to hear Hugh's voice soften. 'Oh, Trixie, she's a gem above price.'

'I've always thought so. But of course, she's my daughter.'

'And a credit to you. What? Wait a minute—' His tone had gone cold and formal again. I heard a tearing and rustle of paper.

'By the sheerest coincidence,' he said, 'a note has just been handed to me. Thank you, Cressida.' His voice was cold enough to have deep-frozen any normal woman. 'Please wait for me outside. I'll be with you as soon as I've finished this private call.' There was a silence long enough to allow someone to leave a room.

'What do you suppose, Trixie?' His voice was still icy. 'It's from the kidnappers. It seems that they want two hundred thousand pounds for the safe return of my children. If I do not pay them, or if I notify the police, I may never see the children again. Two hundred thousand pounds, a nice round number . . .' His tone grew thoughtful. 'That's one hundred thousand pounds per child. Does that sound like the going rate to you?'

'Hugh—Hugh—don't do anything rash!'

'I believe I *will* come over to see you, after all. In fact, we *both* will.'

'Hugh? Hugh?' I clicked the cradle frantically. He had hung up. When I dialled back, I got a busy signal. I dialled and re-dialled, still getting that endless busy signal. I had to assume that they had left the receiver off the hook, probably so that the 'kidnappers' would think that the line was engaged and thus keep their revenge in check.

I hoped Hugh was as forbearing. I would not like to be in Cressida's shoes. Nasty though she was, I had an uneasy suspicion that Hugh—once aroused—could equal any fiendishness she could devise. Once again, I recalled that Producers had to have a streak of steel to survive. And Hugh had not only survived, he was at the top.

'Are you planning to spend the rest of your life on that telephone?' Evangeline inquired from the doorway. 'I'm only asking because poor dear Julian has to ring through to his station to see if he's required on duty tonight.'

I would have thought he'd have already known that, but perhaps this was the English equivalent of a weekend guest sending himself an urgent telegram to return home at once. Evangeline could be quite overpowering in undiluted doses —even for the most devoted biographer.

'All right, all right.' I handed the receiver to Julian Singer and got the full force of his pleading look as Evangeline settled into a chair and gave every indication that she was going to stay and listen to his call.

'It's getting dark.' I began moving around the room, switching lamps on, leaving the one beside the telephone until last. 'It gets dark so early here, especially on grey days.'

'The nights are drawing in.' Taking his cue from me, Julian delayed dialling. His corner was filled with shadows now and he would not be able to see the dial clearly. 'And the forecast is for frost before morning.'

It was as well that the children weren't marooned in the garden tonight.

The back door slammed. It was getting too dark—and perhaps too chilly—for the archery lesson to continue. After a moment, Trevor's enthusiastic voice could be heard, although not what he was saying.

'Who's that?' Evangeline recognized it as an unfamiliar voice.

'That's Trevor,' I said soothingly. 'A very nice boy I met last night at the Harpo.' I decided to skip over the part about his being a waiter. 'He brought me flowers and Martha has been helping him with a new project.'

'This place is worse than Grand Central Station in its heyday,' Evangeline complained.

As though to underline her remark, the doorbell began ringing insistently.

'*Now* what?'

'You answer it, would you, Evangeline?' I began sliding towards the kitchen. 'I must just talk to Martha for a minute.'

Julian began dialling to demonstrate that he was too busy to be pressed into service.

'Really!' Evangeline pulled herself to her feet and glared at us both. The doorbell paused a moment, then pealed louder than ever. She transferred her fury to the unknown caller. 'Have a bit of patience, can't you?'

She stamped through the front hall, almost on my heels. I got out of her way and lingered at the far end of the hall to see who was going to get the full blast of her temper.

'Not again!' She tried to slam the door in someone's face, but that someone was too fast for her.

'I said I would return. Did not dear Julian give you the message?' Griselda brushed past Evangeline and stood triumphant in the hallway.

'Yes, but I'd hoped he'd got the message wrong.' Evangeline held the door ajar, as though also hoping Griselda might be induced to leave. She ought to have known better.

'We will talk now!' Griselda marched down the hallway and paused to drape herself across the doorway while she surveyed the living-room. 'But dear Julian is still here!' she exclaimed in delight. 'How fortuitous!'

'He's just leaving,' Evangeline said quickly, coming up behind her. 'He has to work tonight.' She looked at Griselda's protruding derrière and, for a moment, her foot twitched.

'How terrible!' Griselda released her hold on the door frame and launched herself into the room. 'I did not know they were such slave drivers in this country.'

'Not at all! I mean—' Sergeant Singer was obviously torn between defending his career choice and protecting his line of retreat. 'I mean, it's a question of shifts. I—I've been on the day shift for a while now; it's time I took a night shift and gave one of the other chaps a chance to have a night off. In fact, I'm afraid I must be leaving now—'

'I've already told her that.' Evangeline's slitted eyes told *him* that he was getting a bit too shifty. 'Run along—and remember me to Superintendent Who-Ever.'

'Yes. Of course.' He would do no such thing; the mere idea brought him out in a cold sweat. Superintendent Heyhoe was trying to forget. Sergeant Singer almost ran from the house.

I had followed Evangeline and Griselda back into the living-room and was trying to look as though I had been there all along. It didn't work.

'We won't keep you, Trixie.' Evangeline turned a laser-beam glare on me. 'I know you're anxious to talk to Martha.'

'It can wait,' I said blithely. 'Since Griselda has something important to say to us—'

'Only to me, I believe.' Evangeline looked to Griselda for confirmation.

'Does it matter?' Griselda shrugged. 'You will tell her anyway . . . eventually.'

It was true. I kept smiling. Evangeline kept glaring.

'We'll go up to my study,' Evangeline decided abruptly. 'Just you and I. Trixie has other things to do right now.'

'Heaps,' I agreed. Turnabout was fair play. I'd give them time to get well into their conversation, then I'd go upstairs and look for *my* lorgnette.

'We must agree the vital points—' Evangeline could shoo Griselda up the stairs, but she could not prevent her from talking as she went. 'There are so few of us left who share memories of the great days, the momentous events—'

'Turn right at the landing and go down the little hallway,' Evangeline directed firmly.

'We hold the answers to mysteries that have defeated the police, puzzled generations. The world is waiting for our revelations. We must agree what we shall tell them.'

'Are you suggesting . . .' Evangeline spoke in her most Ethel Barrymore voice. She had paused ominously half way up the stairs and was staring at Griselda's retreating back. It could have been a scene from *The Spiral Staircase*. Except that the staircase wasn't spiral and—unfortunately—there was no villain lurking in the dark at the top of the staircase to strangle Griselda.

'Are you suggesting that we *cook* our books?'

'I suggest—' Griselda pivoted at the head of the stairs, one hand high on the wall, the other reaching for a door frame that wasn't there—'we decide which story each of us will reveal. We will not reveal the same ones. We must also decide how much to tell . . .' She paused and looked down on Evangeline patronizingly. 'Of course, after one of us has died, the other will be free to give *her* version of the events.'

Evangeline had been watching too much English television of late, especially the soccer games. She lowered her head and moved rapidly up the stairs. For a terrible moment, I thought she was going to head-butt Griselda right in the midriff.

Maybe Griselda thought so, too. She dropped her arms and retreated suddenly.

'Evangeline,' I called warningly. 'Shall I bring you some tea?'

'How kind of you, Trixie.' She paused in her headlong charge and glared down at me. 'But don't go to any trouble. Nothing elaborate. Just a little something laced with cyanide will do.'

'Evangeline—' But she was already following Griselda down the upper hallway, the light of battle in her eyes.

'Evangeline—'

'I, of course . . .' Griselda's fading voice drifted back to me, 'shall tell of the unfortunate incidents on Job Farraday's last American picture . . .'

So Job Farraday had refused to pay up, had he? A door slammed, cutting off further revelations and sending its reverberations throughout the whole house.

'Oh dear!' I discovered that I was wringing my hands. 'Oh dear!' Ought I to follow them? Would I really prevent mayhem, if I did? Or would my presence simply incite Evangeline to further heights of violence? Why couldn't Griselda have been born with the sense God gave geese? While I dithered and contemplated these eternal questions, the doorbell rang. Viciously. That *must* be Hugh.

It was, although I hardly recognized him, nor the white-faced woman he pushed into the hallway ahead of him.

'Good evening, Trixie,' he said forbiddingly. 'I'm sorry I'm a little later than I planned. However, I had a bit of difficulty with . . . certain arrangements.' He gave her another shove and she plummeted across to the foot of the stairs and caught herself on the stair rail to keep from falling. 'I trust all is well?'

'Oh yes, yes!' I was aware that I was burbling, trying not to notice that Cressida was terrified, that Hugh was in a towering rage. 'Couldn't be better.'

Just then, Martha laughed. It was a carefree bubbling laugh, of the sort I hadn't heard from her in years. A male laugh joined in, gurgling and triumphant; Trevor, delighted with the progress of his archery lesson. Although anyone with a suspicious nature might interpret it in quite a different way.

Hugh quivered and stared at me accusingly.

'It's only Trevor.' I decided against letting him worry.

The poor devil had enough on his mind. 'The lesson is over and Martha's giving him tea in the kitchen. You can smell the allspice cookies—she made them herself.'

Hugh sniffed obediently and brightened. 'They smell delicious. She made them herself? Starting from scratch?'

'Not a packet or a frozen ingredient in sight. They're her own recipe, too. She's always inventing recipes. She loves cooking.'

'How *bourgeois!*' I had forgotten Cressida until she sneered.

'Maybe.' I wasn't going to let her get away with that. 'But if she had any children, she'd damned well know where they were at night! If that's *bourgeois*, there's a lot to be said for it!'

'You told her!' She whirled on Hugh accusingly. 'You *know* the kidnappers said not to tell anyone or we'd never see the children again. You haven't—' genuine fear gleamed in her eyes—'you haven't notified the police, too, have you?'

He ignored her and raised an eyebrow at me.

'Still sleeping,' I told him.

'What?' She turned back to me. She was quick on the uptake, I'll give her that. 'You mean you've found them? Oh, thank heavens! My babies are safe! Where are they? Let me see them!'

But disappointment shadowed her eyes. She would much rather have seen the ransom money she'd been trying to con out of Hugh.

'You can see them later,' Hugh said. 'I don't want them disturbed now. They've had a bad night—sleeping rough!'

'Oh!' Cressida's eyes widened; she watched Hugh warily. 'How . . . how did that happen?'

'Nova turfed them out of the taxi in order to drive Trixie to the Harpo. Then, despite being told not to, she waited for Trixie. She stayed away so long that the children gave her up and wandered off.'

'So it was all your fault!' Cressida blazed at me.

'We know whose fault it was,' Hugh said coldly. 'Leave Trixie out of this.'

The telephone rang. I was very happy to leave them to it while I went into the living-room to answer. I was not so happy to hear Hugh's next words.

'Go with Trixie.' Hugh spoke in a voice of cold command that brooked no argument. 'I'll speak to you later.'

'Hello?' I tried not to listen to the reluctant footsteps following in my wake.

'Trixie, baby! Howya doin'?'

'Job? Job Farraday?' What did he want?

'Gee, Trixie, it was great seeing you last night. Just like old times. You're still looking great, kid.'

'Thank you. It was good to see you again, too.' Especially when I didn't have to work with him. Ghostly bunions and blisters were even now throbbing on my feet at the sound of his voice.

'Say, listen, Trixie—' He evidently felt that he had spent enough time on the social preliminaries. 'I was wondering. You haven't seen Grisly lately, have you?'

'Oh, Trixie!' Trevor swept into the room, impulsively grabbed me and planted a large kiss on my cheek. 'Trixie, I'll never be able to thank you enough. Thank you! Thank you! I've got to report for duty at the Harpo now, but I'll see you tomorrow. Thank you again!'

I gathered the lesson had gone well.

'Trixie?' Job was plaintive at the other end of the line. 'What the hell's going on there? Are we still connected?'

'Yes, Job. Sorry, I was just saying goodbye to a guest.'

'Not Grisly? I mean, Griselda. Von Kirstenberg.'

'I know who you mean by Grisly. No, someone else was leaving; Grisly's still here. We have a houseful at the moment.' Cressida was glowering at me from a corner. 'Sit down, Cressida!'

'Is Cressida there, too? Hey, I'm with a bunch of people who've been trying to get hold of her for weeks—'

'She isn't staying long,' I said hopefully.

'Hang on to her! Hang on to Grisly, too! I've got to talk to them. It's important, believe me.'

'I won't guarantee anything—' If Cressida wanted to leave, I certainly wasn't going to detain her.

'You can do it! I'm not far away. I'll be right over. Hang on to both of them until I get there!' He slammed down his receiver.

I flinched, but held on to my own receiver. If I replaced it, I would then be trapped into a conversation with Cressida.

'Do you think so, Job?' I asked the humming line.

'I suppose you think you're clever!' Cressida snarled.

'Excuse me, Job.' Just in case I hadn't been discovered, I put my hand over the mouthpiece and looked at Cressida with gentle reproof. 'You said something, dear?'

'You heard me!' She lunged forward and slammed her hand down on the telephone cradle, disconnecting me.

'Oh dear.' I sighed and turned to face her. She had been working herself into a fury. Since Hugh wasn't available, she was going to unleash it on me.

'Would you like a cup of tea?' I made one last vain effort to avert the flood.

She told me what I could do with my tea. I pretended I hadn't heard her.

Fortunately, it made her madder than anything else I could have thought of.

'You and your precious daughter!' She was working herself into incandescence. 'Sneaking over here, worming your way into Hugh's confidence—I suppose you think you're clever!'

'Not as clever as you.' There had been the ring of truth

about her words—only the cast list was wrong. It was all coming clear to me.

'*You* wormed your way into Evangeline's confidence. You approached her after all that publicity last month, after Hugh and Martha had become engaged. You talked her into appearing in that frightful film, so that you could be in and out of this house—trying to make trouble between Martha and Hugh.'

'It's going to be a wonderful film! And that ghastly daughter of yours has no right to be here in the first place. Interfering! Trying to take Hugh away from me—'

'You haven't got him!' I couldn't let that pass unchallenged. 'You divorced him years ago.'

'That means nothing! We'll always be bound together— by the children.'

'Ah yes, the poor little kidnapped darlings.' I looked at her thoughtfully. That was all I did. I didn't even say another word. But it seemed that I'd said enough.

'You think you can use them against me! I'm on to your tricks! Let me tell you—' She took a deep breath and raved on. And on.

It was a full-fledged tantrum, worse than any I'd ever seen a movie brat throw—and I'd seen a few in my time. She'd tried to pull a fast one, been caught—and now it was everybody's fault but hers.

Her behaviour was fuelled by fear, of course. She'd gone too far—and she knew it. Hugh might just possibly have forgiven her for losing track of the children, but to have tried to cash in on their absence with that phoney ransom demand was beyond the pale. If Hugh were to change his mind about going to Court, surely he could get custody of the children on the strength of that alone.

'You think you're so clever—' A full five minutes later, Cressida had begun repeating herself. I wished Hugh would come and take her away. I don't know why he'd brought her here in the first place. But I had better things to do than stand here and listen to her rantings.

'Yes, that's very interesting, dear,' I said. 'But I've got to make some tea for Evangeline and Griselda. You're sure you won't have a cup?'

'And she's another! Both of them! All of you! Playing the male game. Letting them turn you into female stereotypes —imitations of women!'

I smiled blandly and moved towards the door. She dodged in front of me, blocking my exit.

'You don't want to hear the truth! You're afraid of the truth! You want to go on in your own cutesy-poo way—' Suddenly her blank features rearranged themselves into a grotesque simper. She tossed her head, threw out her arms, and broke into a parody of a tap dance routine. She threw herself around like a whirling dervish, without control, without really knowing what she was doing, dancewise, but I could see that it was a fairly clever—and cruel—imitation of me in my early days.

'And that other one! The *Grande Dame*—' She stopped abruptly, tossed her hair off her face and drew herself up, mimicking Evangeline's regal carriage. She raised her eyebrows, tilted her head back, and looked down on me as though from a great height.

'You're good,' I couldn't resist saying. 'You're very good.'

She was. She could project the essence of her victim with just a few movements. Given proper make-up and a few wigs, she could have herself a fabulous cabaret act. What a pity she'd banned any form of glamour from her life. She could have been one of the greats, might still be—if anyone could get her off this feminist kick and back into the mainstream of show business.

'You know—' I braced myself to suggest it—'you ought to—'

'And that other one!' She was beyond hearing me. 'She's

the worst of all! Glamour Girl!' She spat the words out as though they were obscene. I decided not to mention my bright idea just then.

'The falseness—' She rearranged her pale mobile features, shook her head again so that her hair fell over her shoulder, and minced over to the doorway.

'She's a bitch with one trick! The blonde mane, the powder and paint, and she thinks all she has to do is—' Cressida whirled in the doorway and tilted one hip, one hand high on the door jamb, the other low on the opposite door jamb, in Griselda's favourite pose. Except for the featureless face—and a bit of make-up could change that —she was the image of Griselda.

The window across the room suddenly shattered. I turned towards it, scarcely registering a strange humming sound in the air. My first thought was that someone had hurled a brick through the window.

'*Uuuh!*' The explosive sound from Cressida and the thud sounded simultaneously. I turned back to her.

Her eyes, wild and terrified, stared pleadingly into mine. Her hands groped feebly at her breast . . . at the still-quivering arrow pinning her to the door.

CHAPTER 11

I drew a deep breath but, just before I screamed, I remembered the children sleeping across the hallway. They must not be awakened to the nightmare of seeing their mother skewered to the door.

I let the breath out again in a tiny whimper, which was echoed by Cressida.

As I stepped forward to try to help her, her hands dropped limply to her side and her eyes glazed over. A tiny trickle of blood ran down from one corner of her mouth. A deep crimson stain 'was spreading out around the shaft of the arrow, as though marking the centre of the target it had pierced.

There was nothing more anyone could do for Cressida.

'No,' I heard myself whisper bleakly. 'Oh no!' Then there were more whimpering noises, but I couldn't stop myself. It was just too awful and, if I didn't whimper, I'd scream.

I couldn't stay here another moment. I couldn't force myself to reach around Cressida's body and open the door into the hallway, either. I'd have to go out the other way, through the little study that had been turned into a dressing-room for me.

With an apologetic nod, I sidled past Cressida and ran from the room. Not until I had shut the dressing-room door and was leaning against it did it occur to me that someone might still be prowling outside in the underbrush with another arrow strung into position, waiting for the next target.

I suddenly became very reluctant to turn on the light.

But it was an accident. It had to have been. Martha and Trevor must have left the bow and arrows out in the garden after they had finished the lesson and—

And somebody just passing by had seen them and decided to try his hand at the game?

Or had the children awakened and wandered out into the garden and— But that was unthinkable. It was their mother who had been killed.

Dazedly, I rubbed my forehead and tried to think straight.

Half an hour ago this house had been teeming with people. Where was everybody now? I had to tell them what had happened. I couldn't let someone open the living-room door and walk in to find—

The door! I became aware that I was still leaning against the dressing-room door, just as Cressida had leaned against the other door in the moment before being pinioned to it.

I pushed myself away from the door and skittered across the tiny room into the sanctuary of my own bedroom. But I didn't feel safe there, either, with the glass carbuncle of the conservatory opening off the end of it, giving access to the garden.

I hurried out through the deserted kitchen and into Evangeline's room, using the connecting doors and avoiding the hallway. I looked around the empty room, then remembered that Evangeline was upstairs with Griselda in the study she had commandeered from Jasper. But where had Martha and Hugh disappeared to?

Someone had turned on Evangeline's bedside lamp and it glowed softly in the darkness. Beside it, the telephone promised a link with the outside world. Help must be summoned. But what kind of help? It was too late for medical science to do anything.

I sank down on the edge of the bed, my knees giving way, and reached for the telephone. There was a notepad beside it and, printed in extra large numerals so that she could read it without her glasses, was Julian's name and telephone number.

Of course. Julian would know what to do. Besides, telling him would count as notifying the police. I lifted the receiver to eye level and punched out the numbers, hoping that he would be home to take the call. I had lost all track of time.

'Yes?' The voice was guarded, giving nothing away, not even the number I had reached.

'J—Julian?'

'Yes. Who is it?' There was a trace of impatience in the voice. Policemen don't like people who play telephone games.

'J—J—Julian—' I wasn't playing, I just couldn't get my voice under control.

'Trixie? Is that you?' He was suddenly alert, scenting trouble. 'What is it?'

'Ac—Acci- Accident—' I managed to gasp out. 'Sh—
Sh—' Suddenly my mouth and throat had gone dry. All
that came out was a squeak. 'She—ee—ee's dead!'

'Oh my God! How? What happened?'

'Can't . . . talk . . .' As I dropped the phone back into its
cradle and collapsed against the pillows, I heard him shout
faintly:

'I'll be right there!'

I closed my eyes and took a count of ten. Then twenty. At
thirty, I opened my eyes again. At forty, I swung my feet
to the floor. At fifty, I was up and moving again, still feeling
punch-drunk.

I opened the door into the hallway and stood listening to
the silence. On the plus side, it meant that the children were
still asleep; on the minus side, it meant that I was going to
have to step out into a deserted hallway, not knowing what
might be lurking there.

But the danger had come from outside the house, I
reminded myself. True. But it was still against my better
judgement when I stepped out into the hallway.

As though to prove me right, there was a creak at the
head of the stairs, then another. Someone was coming
down.

'Evangeline?' I moved to the foot of the stairs and looked
up.

'Evangeline is impossible!' Griselda stalked down the
stairs in a fury.

'She always was,' I agreed absently, listening for any
sound from the room where the children were sleeping. I
gathered that Griselda had lost the battle. Under any other
circumstances, the thought would have cheered me.

'I go now!' Griselda stalked past me towards the front
door. 'I shall return when she is in a better mood.'

'Yes,' I said, then: 'NO! STOP! Don't go out there!'

'What?' She turned towards me, puzzled. 'Trixie, are you all right?' She frowned, the puzzlement turning to concern as she saw my face. 'What is the matter with you?'

'I—I'm all right.' I knew I couldn't look it. I had begun shaking and my teeth were chattering. Delayed shock was catching up with me.

'Trixie—' Griselda tried to put her arm around me and lead me towards the living-room. 'Come and sit down.'

'STOP!' I croaked again. 'Don't go in there!'

'What insanity is this?' Her first charitable impulse gave way to irritation as I shook off her consoling arm. 'Are you having a fit? Does this happen often?'

'Wait a minute—' I sank down on the lowest stair. 'Just stay here a minute. Or two.' I fought to get my nerves under control.

'Shall I call someone? Can you be left alone? Are there pills you should take?' Griselda was still trying to be helpful, although still with that undertone of irritation.

'No pills. It's nothing like that. I just—' I broke off. How could I tell her that I had just realized that Cressida had been killed in the midst of doing an impersonation of *her?* If it hadn't been an accident, then—

'You look better,' Griselda said unconvincingly. 'I must go now. I have an appointment.'

'NO!' I shrieked as she started for the door again. I could not let her go out there. If the killer were still lurking around, he might see her and finish the job he thought he had already done.

'What is it? Shall I call Evangeline to you?'

'Yes. No. Not yet—' I wanted to talk to Evangeline— but alone. 'I'll go up and see her myself. You wait here.'

'Why?' It was a reasonable question, but one I could not reasonably answer.

'Just wait,' I pleaded, struggling to my feet. 'I'll be right down. Then I'll explain.'

'I suppose I must humour you—' She started for the living-room.

'NO! Not in there!'

'Not out. Not in there. Where shall I wait, then?' Her exasperation gave way to curiosity. 'Explain what?'

'Why don't you wait in the kitchen?' I suggested. 'You could make yourself a cup of tea.'

'You are mad,' she said flatly, but she started down the hallway towards the kitchen.

'And *stay* there,' I called after her, not trusting her a bit. If she went prowling, she'd get a nasty shock—and it would be her own fault. I hadn't time to worry about her further.

Slowly, I mounted the stairs. The temporary respite provided by the argument with Griselda was over and I could hear my teeth chattering again. My knees still felt unreliable and I leaned heavily on the stair rail.

I hesitated before knocking on the study door, hearing voices and thinking that Evangeline must have someone in there with her. If Hugh and Martha were inside, I didn't want to go in. Let the police break the news to Hugh, it was more than I felt able to cope with.

Then I remembered that Martha was not on speaking terms with Evangeline and certainly wouldn't be visiting her. One of the kids from upstairs perhaps; I could chase them out before telling Evangeline. I tapped on the door and opened it.

'Oh, it's you.' Evangeline switched off the tape-recorder. 'Did you get rid of her?'

'I—Sh—She—ee—' The question took my breath away and I was back to squeaking again. 'She—ee—e's dead!'

'Good Lord! You didn't have to go that far. Simply kicking her down the front steps would have been sufficient.'

'I didn't do it!'

'You're innocent!' Evangeline backed me immediately.

'Of course you're innocent. And we'll get the best mouth-piece in town to prove it.'

'Evangeline!' The scream I had been repressing threatened to take over. 'This isn't a scene from *Frails in Jails*. It's real! She's really dead! Downstairs! In *our* living-room!'

'Sit down.' Evangeline peered at me closely and crossed to the desk, pulling open the bottom drawer. There were clinking noises and she returned with a small glass. 'Drink this.'

I sipped at the brandy while she returned to the desk and poured a drink for herself. It steadied me and I was interested to learn that she kept a decanter stashed away up here, too.

'Now—' she sat down opposite me and raised her glass. 'What did she do to annoy you? She's been infuriating me all afternoon, but I held my temper. You were only with her for about five minutes, what on earth did she say to you?'

'Are you talking about Griselda?' The brandy was working and I realized we were at cross purposes. 'There's nothing wrong with Griselda. She's downstairs in the kitchen now. She's fine.'

'Pity,' Evangeline sighed. 'Getting rid of Griselda would have sorted out a lot of problems.'

'For a lot of people,' I agreed. 'No one would ever have to worry about her memoirs again.'

'Wait a minute—' Evangeline stiffened. 'Then who *is* dead?'

'Cressida Garrick-Erving.'

'Cressida?' Evangeline stared at me accusingly. 'You never wanted me to play that part,' she said bitterly.

'Evangeline, I did not kill anyone.'

'And her demise will remove Martha's scruples about being a second wife and following in the footsteps of a famous actress—' My dear friend continued to build the case against me. 'She and Hugh can carry on with the wedding now.'

'*Do* remember to tell all that to the police, won't you?' I snarled. 'It would be a shame if they missed out on any motives.'

'We'll get you the best jury money can buy.' Evangeline got up and took my empty glass for a refill, not neglecting her own. 'Don't worry, Trixie. We'll beat this rap.'

I've never been able to decide whether she does it on purpose or not but, between the brandy and sheer irritation at her, I had stopped shaking and my teeth no longer sounded like castanets.

'What happened?' She handed me my glass.

'She—Someone—' I closed my eyes and shook my head, trying to dislodge the vision that had suddenly filled my mind.

'Never mind. I'll go and see for myself. The living-room, I believe you said.'

'Don't use the hall door—' I got up and followed her. 'Go round the long way.'

She threw a searching look over her shoulder, but made no further comment. Nor did I. Silently, I trailed her down the stairs.

We had just reached the bottom step when Griselda came reeling down the hallway. She halted as she reached us and stood glaring at me. Then she snatched my glass and drained it in a single swallow.

'I told you to stay in the kitchen,' I said righteously.

'You should have said why,' she gasped. She eyed Evangeline's glass, but Evangeline was clutching it jealously, already suspecting that her need was going to be greater than Griselda's.

'Through my bedroom—' I began to lead the way when the doorbell rang behind us.

'Don't let them ring again!' I whirled about and dashed to answer. 'They mustn't wake the children!'

'Children?' Griselda looked about wildly. 'What children?'

I wrenched the front door open and Sergeant Julian Singer erupted into the hall.

'I've called Heyhoe,' he blurted out. 'The rest of them are on the way. Where is she?'

'In the living-room,' I said, but he had lost interest.

'Oh!' He had spotted Evangeline. 'Thank God! Thank God!' He advanced upon her. 'I thought—' He threw his arms around her and clutched her to him. 'I thought—'

'Why, Julian!' Evangeline was unable to save her brandy, it spilled down the back of Sergeant Singer's mufti. 'Dear boy, what on earth—?'

'You're safe!' His voice was muffled, his face pressed into the side of her neck. 'Thank God you're safe!'

'How touching,' Griselda sneered. 'What it is to have a collaborator! Such devotion!'

'And you're all right, too,' Julian said, with considerably less enthusiasm. 'And you—' He turned his head and looked at me. 'Then who—?'

'This way . . .' I started down the hallway again, leading the parade. Well, most of it. Griselda lagged behind and I couldn't find it in my heart to blame her.

'Griselda, why don't you stay here?' I suggested. 'The rest of the police will be arriving any minute. You can open the door before they wake the children.'

'Children? Children? What is this children?' She looked down at the floor wildly, as though she equated children with mice. 'Do you speak of Martha?'

I didn't bother to answer, but Evangeline picked up on the question—she would!

'Where *is* Martha?'

'She's around,' I said vaguely, glaring at her when Julian

wasn't looking. Fortunately, he was too intent on discovering what had happened to notice any byplay. I hoped I didn't look as worried as I felt. Martha was around . . . somewhere . . . and so was Hugh. And the woman who stood between them had just been killed.

At the kitchen, I faltered and fell back. I couldn't go into the living-room and face . . . *that* again.

'Sit down for a minute.' Evangeline caught my arm and lowered me into a chair. Less from sympathy, I suspected, than from a desire to postpone facing the horror herself.

'Both of you stay here,' Julian directed masterfully. 'I'll check this out for myself.'

'Dear boy . . .' Evangeline murmured. 'How kind of you.' Her new-found feminist principles melted away like the snows of winters past. Sisterhood notwithstanding, there is a lot to be said for being a female chauvinist sow when the going gets rough. If Great Big Mans is prepared to charge forward and do all the dirty work, then I, for one, am prepared to lean back and flutter my eyelashes and coo in admiration.

'Trixie needs me—' Evangeline was fluttering enough for both of us. 'She's so overwrought. I'll just put the kettle on.'

Cressida would have called it the conditioning of our generation; we'd call it just plain common sense. Besides, look where her feminist principles had got her.

'That's right.' Sergeant Singer seemed to grow taller and broader. 'You ladies stay here. I'll take care of this.'

He strode off purposefully, not even glancing back over his shoulder, so that Evangeline's trusting *Waif of the Klondike* (when the hero hurled her on to the dog-sled and whipped up the huskies to outrun the crevasse opening up behind them) expression was totally wasted.

'Oh, well.' She sighed and shrugged. 'You don't really want a cup of tea, do you?'

'I'd rather have another brandy,' I said honestly. 'Griselda took mine.'

'So she did. And Julian spilled mine. Never mind, we'll give dear Julian a few minutes to compose himself, then we'll go in and get the brandy. He'll probably be in need of some himself, by then.'

'I don't want to go back into that room.' I was still being honest. 'And I don't think he's allowed to drink on duty.'

'Who's that?' Evangeline was peering out of the kitchen window. 'There's someone in the garden. Are those children out there again?'

'Get out of sight!' I pushed her away from the window. 'It may be the killer!'

'There are two of them—' Evangeline shook me off. 'Does he have an accomplice?'

'How should I know?' But it didn't seem likely. Emboldened by the thought, I risked taking a peek.

A large shapeless mass was advancing upon the house. As it drew nearer, I could see that it was Martha and Hugh, arms around each other's waists, her head on his shoulder.

'It's Martha and Hugh,' I reported. 'Thank goodness, they've made up. They've got their arms around each other.'

'How sweet,' Evangeline said coldly. *Hello, Middle-Aged Lovers . . .'* she began to sing under her breath.

'Oh no! They're coming here!'

'Where else would they go?' Evangeline suddenly realized what I meant. We gazed at each other in consternation.

'I can't tell them!' I said wildly. 'I can't!'

'And I'm not going to!'

As one, we turned and ran from the kitchen.

CHAPTER 12

We collided with Sergeant Singer, who was blocking the dressing-room doorway and moaning softly to himself. 'Cressida Garrick-Erving . . . oh no . . . Cressida Garrick-Erving . . .'

'I told you it was,' I said tartly.

'But she's still young. She had so much to give the world.'

This wasn't the moment to disagree with him, but I didn't think a feminist version of *King Lear* was something the world was waiting for impatiently. If you ask me, the world had had a lucky escape—and so had Evangeline.

'You're in the way!' Evangeline gave him a sharp jab in the small of the back, propelling him into the room. She trotted in briskly behind him, not glancing towards Cressida until she had the brandy decanter grasped firmly in her hand.

'Oh . . .' she said faintly. Her knuckles whitened, so did her face.

I tried not to look in that direction. I concentrated on closing the dressing-room door behind us, to delay Martha and Hugh a little if they came looking for us.

'The hall door should be locked—' I gave Sergeant Singer an imploring look. 'We don't want anyone coming in that way and—'

He shuddered, but he got the message. He went over and, reaching past Cressida's slumped body, snicked down the latch on the Yale lock. Now no one could dislodge the body by inadvertently rushing into the room.

'Here.' Evangeline thrust a glass of brandy into his hand and he had absent-mindedly swallowed half of it before his better judgement reasserted itself.

'I'm on duty,' he gasped. 'Superintendent Heyhoe will kill me!'

'Nonsense, dear boy, you weren't officially on duty until you saw the body. How is the Superintendent to know when you had the drink?' Evangeline handed me my glass and took a thoughtful sip from her own. 'Don't worry, I'll explain it to him.'

'Oh no!' That was even worse. 'No, no, don't bother. I mean—' He meant: one word from her and Heyhoe would throw the book at him. 'It will be all right. Just don't say anything—*please!*'

'All right, but if you have any trouble with the Superintendent, just send him to me.'

Sergeant Singer shuddered involuntarily and, on second thoughts, finished his brandy. It was going to be a long night.

He didn't know how long. Out of the corner of my eye, I saw the door from my quarters begin to open. I rushed across the room and hurled myself against it, holding it shut.

'Mother—?' Martha rapped on it anxiously. 'Mother, are you in there?'

'Keep out!' I said. 'I mean, I'll be right out. Wait there.'

'Mother, let us in. We have something to tell you.'

Not half as much as I had to tell them.

'Mother—' She rapped on the door again.

'In a minute,' I called desperately. It was a silly thing to say. Things weren't going to improve in a minute.

'Mother—'

'Never mind,' Hugh said. 'We'll slip out and buy some champagne. She can join the celebration when we get back.'

'Most unwise,' Evangeline murmured.

'No—don't!' I had already come to that conclusion myself. 'For God's sake, don't do that!'

I stepped away from the door. In the distance I could

hear the urgent wail of a police siren. We couldn't keep the lid on this any longer.

'All right,' I said. 'Come in.'

'Mother, what on earth—?' Martha stumbled into the room as I stopped holding the door. 'It's freezing in here. Why don't you shut the window? Oh!' She looked more closely. 'Mother, who broke the window?'

'That is the question,' Evangeline said grimly.

Hugh had caught Martha's arm as she stumbled, now he followed Evangeline's gaze and his hand fell away.

'No!' One strangled gasp, then he advanced upon the figure pinioned to the door. He reached out a tentative hand and touched her lightly on one cheek.

'Oh, Mother—not again!' Martha said. Then Hugh moved aside slightly and she saw who it was. 'Oh, Mother!'

'Poor Cressida,' Hugh said brokenly. 'Poor, poor little Cress. You didn't deserve this.'

Outside, the police car raced up the driveway, siren still whooping to ensure that none of the neighbours missed its destination. Detective-Superintendent Heyhoe had done that just to annoy Evangeline, I was sure.

'Really!' He had succeeded. Evangeline crossed to the bay window, carefully avoiding the broken glass from the side panel, and frowned out. 'All that commotion is quite unnecessary.'

'I'd better go and let them in.' Sergeant Singer started from the room, not displeased at an excuse to leave.

'There's no need—' But Sergeant Singer had already escaped.

Martha looked as though she wished she could. She stared helplessly at Hugh, but it was obvious that he no longer remembered that she was in the room. Or that any of us were. He mourned silently beside Cressida, lost in memories and sadness.

Martha drew closer to me, sensing that she could not

reach him—and that it might be wiser not to try. I put my arm around her.

Evangeline poured more brandy, recognizing that it was the only sensible thing anyone could do. Martha accepted the proffered glass abstractedly, still watching Hugh. Evangeline topped up my glass and her own, then, possibly with a view to disposing of the evidence, picked up Sergeant Singer's discarded glass, polished it briskly with her handkerchief, as though removing fingerprints, poured fresh brandy into it and carried it over to Hugh.

At first he tried to wave it away, but Evangeline persisted. He took it and suddenly discovered he needed it.

'That's right.' Evangeline nodded approval, her expression soft and concerned. 'My dear, I wish there were something more we could do.'

Hugh turned away, struggling for control. Heavy footsteps were marching down the hallway on the other side of the door; the vibration set the arrow to quivering horribly.

Martha gave a soft whimper and pressed closer to me, gazing despairingly at Hugh. She wanted to go to him, but was obviously unsure of her welcome from the pain-racked man who had suddenly become a stranger.

'They are in here—' Griselda's voice came from the doorway. 'I do not go in again.'

'That's quite all right, madam, but you won't go far, will you? We'd like to speak to you later.' Detective-Superintendent Heyhoe came into the room.

Frankly, I'd hoped never to see him again—and the feeling was obviously mutual. Evangeline, however, had no such qualms.

'Why, if it isn't Superintendent Who-He,' she said, in pleased surprise.

'It's still Heyhoe, madam.' He ignored her extended hand. This was not a social occasion.

'Of course it is.' Evangeline patted his arm comfortingly.

'And you wouldn't have it any other way, would you?'

He blinked and began to look harassed. Behind him, Sergeant Singer was trying to look as though he had never seen any of us before.

'When did this happen?' Heyhoe stared at the door in distaste, as though the victim had been guilty of a breach of etiquette by allowing herself to be killed in such a grotesque manner.

'I'm not sure. M-maybe three-quarters of an hour ago. Maybe less.' Time had swerved and looped and lost all meaning since that terrible moment when the window had shattered. 'I—I didn't look at my watch.' A sudden shudder racked me.

'So, it was dark, but you hadn't drawn the curtains?'

'No, it didn't seem necessary. No one could see in from the street and we aren't overlooked by anybody—' But tonight, we had been. Someone had lurked outside, looking in, able to see us as clearly as though we had been moving around on a lighted stage set. Someone watching, waiting his chance . . . I knew I would never leave the curtains undrawn again.

'It was an accident—' I tried to quiet the horrors in my own mind. 'It *must* have been.'

'Strange sort of accident.' Superintendent Heyhoe was staring down at the arrow. 'You don't find this sort of weapon just lying around.'

'Actually—' Sergeant Singer's voice seemed to come from him reluctantly—'Actually, I believe there was some archery activity here earlier in the day.'

'Darling,' I pleaded with Martha. 'Trevor *did* take the bow and arrows away with him when he left?'

'No, of course not,' Martha said. 'He's coming back for another lesson in the morning.'

'Then—' I was still pleading—'you brought them into the house and put them away carefully?'

'I was going to.' Martha looked embarrassed. 'But then Hugh arrived and—and I forgot.'

And she and Hugh had gone down into the garden . . . to the swing . . . next to the target we had set up . . . and the bow and arrows. It didn't take a *Happy Couple* script for me to know what Detective-Superintendent Heyhoe's reaction to that was going to be. When he found out.

'I see.' Martha was so transparent that Heyhoe probably did see—or was able to make a good guess. 'So everyone had a few drinks—' His nostrils twitched accusingly as he stared pointedly at the glasses in all our hands. 'The party got a bit out of hand. Someone began fooling around with the bow and arrows—'

'Nothing like that,' Evangeline denied crisply. 'None of us had anything to do with this. We hadn't even had a drink until this happened—then we needed one. For shock, you know. It was a terrible shock.'

'Ah yes, madam.' His gaze lingered on the depleted brandy decanter. 'I seem to recall that you shock quite easily.'

'For God's sake!' Hugh burst out. 'Can't you do something? You can't leave her here like this!'

'All in good time, sir,' Heyhoe said. 'I'm afraid we can't do anything until the SOCO team gets here and goes through its paces.'

'Socco?' Evangeline was intrigued. 'Do you mean these investigations are rated the way *Variety* rates shows? If this is a Socco, what do you consider a Boffola?'

'No, no, Miss Sinclair,' Singer hissed, going formal in the presence of his boss. 'That's S.O.C.O.—Scene of the Crime Officer. It's nothing to do with showbiz slang.'

'Just what—' Heyhoe refused to be diverted, all his attention had centred on Hugh. 'Just what was your relation to the deceased?'

'She's—she was—my ex-wife.'

'Mmm. Didn't I hear somewhere—' he was on sure

ground and he knew it—'that you were engaged to this lady over here?' He indicated a blushing Martha.

'That's right, we were.' Hugh raised his head and looked at Martha dully. 'We are.'

'I see . . .' Heyhoe put a world of meaning into the remark.

'I think you ought to know—' I couldn't let him follow along that track when it was so patently the wrong track. 'Just before she—she was shot, Cressida was doing an imitation of Griselda von Kirstenberg. It was brilliant. Anyone might have been fooled by it. Even someone a lot closer than an archer prowling around outside. She was posing in the doorway, just the way Griselda always does. She looked just like her. From a distance, I'd defy anyone to tell the difference.'

'It's all clear now!' Evangeline said triumphantly. 'That makes perfect sense. *Anyone* would have wanted to kill Griselda!'

'You wouldn't like to be a bit more specific, madam?' Heyhoe's voice was not encouraging. '*Anyone* covers quite a large field.'

'Anyone who ever knew her,' Evangeline amplified obligingly. 'Wait until you've talked with her, then you'll understand.'

'Possibly.' Hevhoe's tone was neutral, but his fleeting expression said: *Oh God! Not another one!* Any conversation with Evangeline left him feeling murderous, a fact of which she was blithely unaware.

The doorbell pealed abruptly and we all jumped.

'There's SOCO,' Sergeant Singer said and started forward. But Griselda was still on sentry duty; we heard her voice raised in greeting, answered by another, deeper voice. After a brief babble of sound, hurrying footsteps advanced upon us the long way round.

'Christ on a pogo stick!' Job Farraday appeared in the

doorway, staring incredulously at the scene before him. 'What the hell is going on here?'

'Job, darling!' Evangeline started forward to meet him, flinging a stage whisper over her shoulder to Superintendent Heyhoe: 'Here's one!'

'One what!' Heyhoe muttered dazedly.

'Suspect!' Evangeline hissed, advancing on Job with a Judas kiss.

'Don't come in.' Heyhoe tried to regain command of the situation. 'What are you doing here? Who are you?'

'I told Trixie I was coming—' He looked to me for confirmation. 'On the telephone, just a little while ago. I'm Job Farraday.'

'That's right.' I had forgotten the conversation with Job. It seemed to have taken place years ago, in another life, another world. 'He's expected.'

'Sure I am.' Oblivious of Heyhoe's command, Job moved into the room, staring at Cressida's body. 'Oh Jesus! What went wrong? Why didn't somebody warn me before I walked in here. You know I've got a bad heart. This coulda given me a coronary.'

'Poor Job,' Evangeline said soothingly. 'You need a brandy.'

'Not here, madam,' Superintendent Heyhoe said. 'We have work to do. Would you kindly move this—' he glanced around distastefully—'this Irish Wake elsewhere. But don't go too far, we'll want to speak to all of you as soon as we're through here.'

'We'll go upstairs,' Evangeline decided. 'Dear Jasper allows me to use his study, he won't mind if we borrow his sitting-room for a while, too.' If he minded, it was too late. Jasper was going to learn that the adage about giving someone an inch and they'll take a mile might have been minted by some formerly unwary person who had had dealings with Evangeline.

Cars had been drawing up outside and, as we went along the hallway, we crossed paths with men carrying ominous-looking black cases and bits of equipment.

'Jeez, Trixie,' Job muttered, 'I told you those incompetent berks would kill someone with those arrows!'

'They didn't!' I rushed to defend Trevor and Martha. It did not surprise me that Job was aware of Trevor's little deception; it was par for the course in our business. 'Martha would never have allowed such an accident to happen.'

'You mean she did it on purpose?'

'Shh!' Why was his voice so loud? 'No, of course not. She didn't do it at all. Nobody—' I broke off, I wasn't making sense. Only too obviously, somebody had.

'This way—' Evangeline tried to chivvy us up the stairs.

Griselda got into the procession, falling into step just behind Evangeline. Her bright beady eyes kept a check on the rest of us, not intending to miss a thing. She was either planning another chapter of her memoirs, or looking for the next likely blackmail victim. I must find an opportune moment to let her know that Cressida had been killed while imitating her. That ought to get it through even her thick skull that she might have tried someone's patience too far.

'Excuse me—' Job had lingered at the foot of the stairs and now he spoke to the young policeman who had taken Griselda's place at the door. 'I wonder if you could do me a favour? I've got some friends coming round to collect me in a little while. Could you call me when they arrive?'

'I'm not sure you'll be able to leave, sir.' The policeman eyed him doubtfully. 'If the Superintendent hasn't finished with you—'

'Well, maybe you could let them come up to see me,' Job bargained. 'I'd like to talk to them. I mean, they all knew Cressida. They were colleagues. They'd worked with her. This is going to be quite a shock to them.'

'I'm not sure—'

'Look.' Job raised his voice, cutting the policeman off. 'It's a reasonable request. I'm an innocent member of the public and I have rights—'

'Shhh, please.' I caught at Job's arm. 'There are children sleeping in there—' I gestured towards Martha's room by the foot of the stairs.

'In fact—' I smiled sweetly at the policeman—'I wanted to ask you to please let me know when they wake up, so that I can come down and get them. We don't want them wandering around the house at a time like this. It would be awful if they should get into the living-room and see—'

The policeman shuddered, he was way ahead of me.

'Kids?' Job was instantly alert. 'Whose? Martha's?'

'Mmm . . .' I was not prepared to go into that, especially not with a police witness. 'We can catch up with old times later, Job. The others will be waiting for us now.'

'Sure, sure,' he agreed hastily. 'And *I'll* be waiting for *my* friends, don't forget.' He glared at the hapless young constable.

'And if the children begin to stir—' I gave the constable a melting smile.

'I'll call you to see to them.' He didn't want to be the one to deal with them. 'Don't you worry.'

'Thank you.' I gave him a final smile, turned and tried to ascend the stairs as majestically as Evangeline.

'Say, Trixie—' My effort was ruined by Job, who grabbed at my arm and pulled me off-balance. 'Whoops! Take it easy!' He caught me as I stumbled, obviously with no awareness that he had been the cause. 'You ought to take more water with it.'

I reminded myself that I couldn't kick him downstairs with the constable watching, gave him an icy glare and shook my arm free.

'Tell me, Job,' I said, before he could blunder vocally any more. 'Who are you expecting?'

I continued quickly up the stairs so that he had to trail after me as he answered.

CHAPTER 13

'The usual crowd—' He sounded a little breathless. 'Roger, Clive, Whit and Posy. I was with them when I rang you. In fact, I'm surprised they weren't here ahead of me. I tipped them off that Cressie was here and they were dying to see her. I had to make another telephone call before I could get away.'

'They didn't come here.' And thank heavens for that. We already had more than we could cope with around here.

'We were going to meet for drinks at that pub in St John's Wood High Street—the one with the Mona Lisa for a pub sign—they call the Third Mrs Gioconda. Then we were going to catch the show at the Hampstead Theatre. It got pretty good reviews and they're planning to transfer it to the West End. I thought I'd look it over with a view to taking an option on the film rights before anyone beat me to it.'

The sitting-room door was ajar and I realized that Job's remarks had been overheard as I pushed the door open and we entered. The others were just a little too casual about the way they accepted us into their midst.

'I thought you were pretty thoroughly tied up in this Robin Hood production,' I said, just to remind everyone of that. Only it was also reminding them of the reason a bow and arrow had been available to a killer. 'I mean—'

'Hey, Trixie, baby—' Job was the only one who hadn't

noticed my gaffe. He was too caught up in his own concerns. 'You mean to say you don't think I can do two things at once? Remember how it was in our heyday? We could turn out a first class Grade B feature in ten, fourteen days. I bet I could still crank one out before Posy's finished the costumes and set designs for the stage production.'

'Things are slower nowadays, Job. They use colour photography, and the Unions don't let you work the actors twenty-two hours a day any more.'

'Maybe, baby—but if I get me some actors who aren't afraid of work, who know how we did it in the old days—' Very carefully, he did not look at anyone else in the room.

Hugh was still sunk in misery, unnoticing. But Evangeline and Griselda had both straightened up and begun to preen themselves. I suddenly wondered what sort of cast the film would require. Job had chased over here because he'd said he wanted a word with Griselda. Had he also intended to have a few words with the rest of us?

'Say—I just got a great idea!' He was a lousy actor. If he'd just thought of the idea, I was Marie Antoinette.

'Why don't we—' his eyes bulged, his face twisted grotesquely in what he obviously thought was a rendition of someone receiving an inspiration—'why don't *we* make a film?'

'I've got a great idea,' I mimicked, in my best Mickey Rooney voice, as in all those High-School-Kids musicals. 'Why don't we put on a show?!!'

I folded my arms and stared challengingly at him. Evangeline and Griselda watched him, wary but receptive. Blast them!

'Sure! That's it! Great idea, Trixie! We can knock one off, sort of, between engagements for you. Maybe even do it in black and white. That's coming back as an art form now.'

'I don't know—' Evangeline murmured, in token resistance. 'We're *supposed* to be doing *Arsenic and Old Lace* in the West End.' She glanced at Hugh, but there was no response.

'I must get back to the States,' Griselda demurred unconvincingly. 'Of course, I might postpone my departure—if this didn't take too great a length of time.'

'With a great set of Old Pros like you girls, how long could it take? One set, good strong storyline, keep it simple, lots of close-ups. We'll rehearse everything before we shoot—'

'Rehearse *what?*' I wanted to know. It was just like Evangeline to consider jumping from the *Queen Leah* frying-pan into Job's beckoning fire.

'This show from the Hampstead Theatre—I'll take you to see it. Let me ring and see if I can get three more tickets—' He started for the telephone.

'I don't think we'll be able to leave the house tonight,' I reminded him. 'You're probably going to miss the performance yourself.'

'True. OK, I'll take you as soon as I can. I promise you, there's three great parts in it. Trust me! Would I do you wrong?'

'You would if you could. Fortunately, *we're* a little too old these days.' I gave him a meaningful look, so that he could wonder whether I'd heard those rumours about the chorus girls.

'Speak for yourself alone!' Griselda said. 'I feel that one is never too old for a challenging experience.' She slunk over to him. 'You interest me strrangely,' she purred, in almost a parody of one of her vamp roles. 'Tell me, how much are you going to pay?'

'Uh—' It was obvious that he hadn't thought that far ahead yet. Either that, or he'd hoped we were going to be too much of the ladies to bring up such a delicate subject.

'Don't worry, we'll come to a good arrangement. Tell you what—I'll give you a piece of the action. You can have a percentage of . . . the net take!'

'The gross take!' Evangeline snapped. She'd been caught like that once—and never again. The producers were still reporting a net deficit while the film was grossing its third fortune on worldwide re-release.

'Personally, I'd settle for a lump sum—up front,' I said. Griselda nodded vehemently.

'Really, Mother!' Martha stormed over to us. She still didn't know what to do about Hugh, but she had never been shy about putting the rest of us in our places.

'How can you? All of you! Right in front of poor Hugh!'

'Darling, I'm sorry.' I was instantly contrite. We all were. Like old fire horses scenting smoke, we had gone galloping off, forgetting about Hugh and what had so recently happened downstairs. Or was that part of it? Martha was still too young to understand the way people needed to reach out for life when confronted by death. And movies were our life.

'We didn't mean any disrespect,' Job said quickly. 'It was just— We got carried away.'

'Well, I suggest you *go* away—all of you!' Martha had never been one to accept an apology gracefully. 'This poor man is in mourning, he should be left in peace.'

'You are right.' Griselda sent him a sympathetic look which went unnoticed. It's doubtful that he even heard Martha's protests on his behalf. He was still too sunk in shock and horror.

'I expected better of you, Mother,' Martha said bitterly. 'If not of Miss von Kirstenberg and . . . and *Miss Sinclair!*'

'All right,' Evangeline said. 'We were just leaving. We'll finish our discussion in the study.'

I was the last one out. I looked back to see Martha take

her rightful place by Hugh's side and put her arms around him at last.

'I'm sorry, madam.' Another policeman barred the door to the study. 'I'm afraid Detective-Superintendent Heyhoe will be needing this room. He'll let you know when he wants to question you.'

'A fine thing!' Evangeline fumed. 'Come along.' She gestured us towards the stairs. 'We'll use my bedroom.' She glared at the young constable. 'I assume I have not yet been dispossessed from my own bedroom?'

'Bot unless someone has been murdered in there, madam.' The young man was made of sterner stuff than Evangeline had thought. He smiled blandly into her most withering glare.

'Hmmph!' She tossed her head, pivoted on her heel and stalked away.

The rest of us were already in full retreat, clustered at the top of the stairs, waiting for her. Barely sparing us a glance, she swept past and descended the stairs. I let the others follow immediately after her and brought up the rear, my ears straining to hear any murmur of voices from the sitting-room. But whatever Martha and Hugh were doing, they were doing it silently.

Evangeline turned at the foot of the stairs, not deigning to notice the policeman standing guard duty at the front door, and led the procession down the hallway. I lagged behind again, this time listening for any sound from the children, but they were silent, too. I began to feel uneasy. They had been sleeping for quite a long time now—and how could they sleep through all this commotion?

The doorbell rang when Evangeline was half way down the hallway and Job Farraday halted and turned back.

'That will be the gang,' he said. He moved to greet them as the policeman opened the door. 'Nice timing, gang!'

But it was Nova and Lucy who stumbled into the hallway, looking as though demons were chasing them, their hair dishevelled and terror in their eyes.

'We were just driving past—' Nova came straight to me. 'And we saw all the cops. What's happened? Have they— Have they found the bodies?'

'What?' Wouldn't you just know that would be the moment when Detective-Superintendent Heyhoe appeared from nowhere with his ears flapping?

'What bodies, madam?' He charged forward eagerly. 'Do you know of more?'

'More?' Nova took a step backwards, beginning to realize that she had opened her mouth and crammed all four feet into it.

She simultaneously became aware that everyone was staring at her and of the state she was in. Evangeline and the others had turned around and come back to the foot of the stairs, where they clustered, watching the new arrivals.

'I'm waiting for your answer, madam,' Detective-Superintendent Heyhoe said coldly.

'Um, er, I just meant . . .' Nova raked a hand through her hair and seemed surprised when it came away with a leaf in it. She looked around wildly, then thrust the leaf deep into a pocket. She was wearing something shapeless and knitted; it probably hadn't been quite so shapeless when she started out, but all the pulled threads and unravelling stitches hadn't helped.

Lucy looked just as bedraggled; she was keeping in the background, trying to restore some order to her own appearance. I made a mental bet that they had been crawling under the bushes and through the undergrowth down by the canal, looking for the children.

'I'm still waiting.' Superintendent Heyhoe was implacable.

'Oh, don't be so silly!' Evangeline snapped. 'There are no more bodies here!'

'There are *always* more bodies here, madam.' Superintendent Heyhoe turned his searching gaze on Evangeline. 'I am simply trying to establish how many more—this time. And where they have been hidden.'

'It must be terrible to have such a suspicious mind,' Evangeline said righteously. 'No wonder you became a policeman. You were unfit for any other occupation.'

'What is he talking about?' Lucy's voice rose on a note of hysteria. 'What other bodies? I mean, why are the police here at all?'

It was unwise of her to have drawn attention to herself. Superintendent Heyhoe took a good long look at her—and did not miss the mud caking her trainers. That did it. His eyes gleamed. I knew that he would not rest until his men had dug up the garden.

'Jesus! Haven't they told you?' Job was one beat behind the conversation, but he made up for it by blundering in regardless. 'Cressida's dead!'

'What?' Both Nova and Lucy shrieked.

'In there—' Job pointed dramatically to the closed door. 'With an arrow through her heart—pinning her to the door.'

'I don't believe it!' Nova said. 'You've gone insane.'

'OK—go and see!'

'Just one moment—' Superintendent Heyhoe moved to intercept them as they started forward. He motioned to his men for reinforcement. 'You can't go in there. We're working in there.' He frowned at Job. 'You ought to know better, sir.'

'Sorry,' Job said. 'I always get carried away with a good scene.'

'Working in there?' Nova looked to me for confirmation. I wished she wouldn't. 'It can't be true! . . . Can it?'

All I could do was nod weakly.

There was a thud as Lucy slid to the floor in a dead faint. I sympathized with her reaction; she'd never be able to find another sucker to peddle that ghastly script to.

'Lu!' Nova cried in anguish. 'Cressie!' More anguished still. She turned first one way, then the other, unable to decide which stricken comrade to go to first.

By this time it was academic, as the policeman on guard duty had her firmly in his grasp. She wasn't going anywhere, although she continued to struggle.

'Pick her up!' Heyhoe ordered, gesturing to Lucy.

'Sir!' the young constable said, obligingly, if desperately. He had his hands full with Nova.

'You pick her up, Job,' Evangeline ordered. 'It's your fault she fainted. You should have broken the news more tactfully.'

'Me? I've got a bad back. If I try to heave her around, you'll have two of us on the floor.'

Superintendent Heyhoe had begun to twitch. He looked around, assessing the situation: Three fairly ancient damsels, whose combined efforts were unlikely to be able to shift a dead weight, even if they felt inclined to try; one fairly young and able-bodied woman who was hysterical and keeping his only available man fully occupied trying to restrain her; and one elderly man who claimed a bad back.

'SINGER!' Heyhoe bellowed. 'SINGER!'

'Sir?' Detective-Sergeant Singer appeared at the end of the hallway, looking wary—as well he might. It was obvious that, in some obscure way, Superintendent Heyhoe felt that Singer was somehow responsible for getting him into this whole situation.

'She does not fall gracefully.' Griselda draped herself over the stair rail and looked disdainfully at the fallen Lucy.

'Why should she, you stupid cow?' Nova defended her friend. 'She's not a bloody actress. She's a writer!'

'Ah.' Griselda nodded sagely. 'That explains it.'

'Singer—' Heyhoe's voice was under tight control—'remove these people! All of them.' He indicated Lucy. 'Start with that one.'

'Sir!' Sergeant Singer almost saluted; he lost the impulse as he looked down at Lucy. 'Is she—?'

'She's alive,' Heyhoe said regretfully. He seemed to feel that there were too many bodies around and that not enough of them were dead.

'You'd better put her in Evangeline's room,' I suggested. 'Everybody's trooping through mine to get in and out of the living-room.'

'The living-room!' Nova twisted afresh in her captor's grasp. 'I've got to go in there. Let me go! I've got to see her. She can't be dead. I'll never believe it until I see her.'

'All right.' Heyhoe nodded to the constable. 'Let her have one quick look. Don't let her touch anything. Then bring her upstairs for questioning.'

The constable ushered Nova down the hallway while Superintendent Heyhoe made his escape up the stairs, leaving Sergeant Singer staring down gloomily at the body on the floor. He did not seem particularly cheered, either, by the fact that it was still breathing. He crouched and tugged at her shoulders, trying to raise her into a sitting position.

'Oooh . . .' she sighed, eyelids fluttering. Abruptly, she was fully conscious and aware of what was happening. 'Take your hands off me or I'll call the police!' she snapped, sitting up.

'Don't be tedious,' Evangeline said. 'He *is* the police.'

'Police—' Memory returned, her eyelids lowered again, she began to sink back towards the floor, realized that Sergeant Singer was still crouched there, ready to catch her, and scrambled awkwardly to her feet.

'Oh!' She stood there swaying. 'Oh, it's coming back to me!' She raised both hands and cupped her head in anguish. 'Cressie! They said she's dead. She isn't—?'

'I'm afraid so,' Evangeline said.

'But she can't be,' Lucy wailed. 'What—what are we going to do now?'

'I don't know what you're going to do,' Evangeline said, 'but I'm going to my room to lie down. I have a terrible headache and—' she glared at Sergeant Singer and me— 'I do not wish to be disturbed.'

Trust Evangeline to pull the rug out from under everybody's feet. That put her room out of bounds—and we couldn't hang around in the front hall all night. Sergeant Singer had already shot a puzzled glance towards Martha's room, as though wondering why we couldn't adjourn in there; he knew Martha was in the upstairs sitting-room with Hugh. He did not know about the children and I'd rather he didn't find out—they could be construed as a further motive for Martha and Hugh to wish to be rid of Cressida. In fact, when the police began sorting things out and adding them up, there were going to be too many motives for Martha and Hugh.

We all watched in varying degrees of chagrin as Evangeline glided down the hallway. Three-quarters of the way down, she threw a graceful wobble, one hand to her head, the other hand reaching out to steady her as she swayed. She was very good at it, but then, she ought to be. I'd watched her rehearse it twenty-seven times before the Director had been satisfied.

Sergeant Singer started forward anxiously, but I put my hand on his arm, stopping him.

Evangeline straightened her eloquent back, lifted her gallant chin, and glided forward again—into the gathering storm of scandal and disgrace.

'Oh,' Sergeant Singer said, enlightened. '*Against the World*.'

'You got it.' I released his arm. Evangeline would have been furious if he'd ruined her scene.

'Oh,' Lucy mourned, 'she'd have made such a great *Queen Leah*. Now what are we going to do?' She answered her own question by bursting into sobs.

Maybe Evangeline *could* have saved that script—but I wouldn't like to bet on it. And I was pretty sure no one else would—especially a Producer risking real money. That meant Lucy could be scratched off the list of suspects. She wouldn't have killed the goose that was about to help her lay the golden egg. That probably went for the rest of the Widow's Mite company; without Cressida as figurehead and moving spirit, they were back to trying to find someone insane enough to take them seriously. And none of them had anything against Griselda.

'Do you think—' Lucy dabbed at her eyes as she sighted a ray of hope—'do you think Evangeline might be willing to finance the film herself? And perhaps you might like to contribute to such a major Art Film?'

'Sorry,' I said cheerfully. 'It wouldn't be possible for either of us.' I'd run into that sort of proposal before and my story was all prepared. 'The men we married left us well provided for, but the funds are held in trusts guarded by a dragon squad of lawyers, who protect us—even from ourselves.'

'Men!' Lucy said bitterly and wept afresh.

Griselda and Job had detached themselves completely from the situation by now and were sitting on the stairs in murmured conversation which seemed to be half-flirtatious —at least on Griselda's part. They might have been sitting out a dance at a party.

A faint air of desperation was beginning to show in Sergeant Singer's manner. Again he cast a puzzled look towards Martha's door. At any moment Superintendent Heyhoe might reappear at the top of the stairs—and he would not be pleased to discover a crowd scene still going on in the front hall. Singer had been ordered to clear the hall.

Poor boy. He'd been so happy helping Evangeline with her autobiography; mixing with us all was his idea of glamour. Now he'd been rudely yanked back on his own side of the fence. Torn between his two loves, the law and the cinema, he was growing more miserable by the minute. Whichever one he did his duty by, the other one was going to hate him. He was in a no-win situation and just beginning to realize it.

A key scraped in the lock. Sergeant Singer whirled as though to stand his ground against advancing hordes.

'Cwumbs!' Gwenda and Des exploded into our midst as though propelled by a whirlwind.

'Cwumbs! What's going on here?'

CHAPTER 14

'I'm sorry, sir.' An unhappy young constable was immediately behind them. 'I couldn't stop them. They say they live here. And they *have* a key . . .'

'It's all right.' Sergeant Singer seemed equally unhappy. 'They *do* live here.' He stared at them glumly; the house was full of unhappy policemen tonight. 'You can go back on guard. Just try to keep any media out.'

'Yes, sir!' The media, the Press, were child's play compared to this lot, the constable's attitude said. He retreated thankfully back to his post.

'Oh, Twixie—' Gwenda hurled herself at me like an overgrown St Bernard puppy. 'Twixie— We peeked thwough the window—' She broke off and buried her head in my shoulder.

'It *is* Cressida, isn't it?' Des was pale grey with a slight shading of green around the gills. 'What happened?'

'It's Cressida,' I confirmed, patting Gwenda's shoulder

absently. What were they doing back so soon? It couldn't be that late, could it?

Gwenda began to cry on my shoulder. Lucy was slumped against the far wall, crying. The constable in charge of Nova came down the hallway, propelling his charge before him. Nova was crying, too.

'We've got to clear this area,' Sergeant Singer said desperately. 'You—' He rounded on the young constable. 'Take her upstairs to Superintendent Heyhoe. And—' he pointed at Lucy—'take her, too!'

'But what happened?' Gwenda sobbed. 'Oh, Twixie—' she gasped for breath as she thought the unthinkable. 'Twixie, is Evangeline all wight?'

'Evangeline is fine,' I said firmly. 'She's lying down.'

'She is lying, yes,' Griselda said. 'Down, I think not.'

The annoying thing was that she was probably right. Evangeline had cornered the market in headaches, but I wondered if it was too late for me to develop some vague malady which would necessitate retreat to a darkened room and peace and quiet whenever crisis threatened.

'What time is it?' It was certainly too late tonight, but the lateness reminded me of another nagging worry.

'It's just past nine,' Gwenda said. 'All the theatre cwowds are in watching the shows, so we decided to pack up early. Besides, it started waining a little while ago. No one's going to hang about on a night like this.'

She *was* a bit damp, now that she mentioned it.

'Gee,' Job said. 'I guess my friends went straight to the theatre. I rang the pub and left a message for them to call for me here, but I guess the message got garbled and they thought they were supposed to meet me at the theatre.'

'Umm, yes.' Sergeant Singer had little interest in Job Farraday's social arrangements, although anyone could have told him that Job was notorious for leaving telephone

messages which were so obscure they were invariably misin-
terpreted. Singer glanced towards Martha's room again.

There were strange noises and urgent cries coming from
behind the living-room door. I guessed that all their pictures
had been taken, their on-the-spot examinations completed,
and that they were now trying to free Cressida's body. That
would account for the muffled cursing; it would not be a
pleasant or an easy job. And, when it was completed, they
would have to carry the body through the front hall and out
to the waiting van.

'We can't stay here.' Sergeant Singer understood the
meaning of the sounds even better than I. He began edging
over to Martha's room. 'Why don't we—?'

'No,' I said quickly. 'I mean, we're supposed to be in the
upstairs sitting-room. That's where Superintendent Heyhoe
will expect to find us when he wants us. Only we—we had
to get out for a little while—' Recklessly, I threw Martha
and Hugh to the wolves. 'Because Hugh needed some
privacy to . . . to compose himself. It's a terrible shock
to find your ex-wife dead like that. But—' I started firmly
for the stairs—'he should have composed himself by
now.'

Griselda and Job jumped up to avoid being trodden on
as I bore down on them, sensing that I was in no mood to
give any quarter. I brushed past them and went up the
stairs, giving a firm lead to the rest. They fell in behind me
and I led the procession into Jasper's sitting-room.

Martha and Hugh were not in there. That was the least
of my concerns at the moment. I had to get out of here,
sneak back downstairs without anyone seeing me—and
check on the children. I know they had been chilled and
exhausted—but could they really have slept the clock
around? Surely they should have been stirring by now. They
were young and healthy . . .

The nagging horror at the back of my mind crept forward

again. Had I overdosed them with the aspirin? Worse, could they possibly be allergic to it? I hadn't thought to ask; I'd just crushed it up and slipped it into their second cup of cocoa, in that calm 'adults know best' assurance. If I had asked them if they wanted any, would they have told me they couldn't take it? That it did awful things to them?

'Twixie, are you all wight? You look so pale.' Gwenda took my arm, steering me to a chair.

'Yes ... I mean, no ... I mean—' I sank into the armchair gratefully. 'I was there when—when the arrow came through the window.' I leaned back and closed my eyes, but the vision of Cressida's skewered, briefly struggling body seemed to be projected against my inner eyelids. I opened my eyes abruptly.

'Cwumbs! No wonder you're pale!' Gwenda was wide-eyed. 'You ought to be lying down like Evangeline. I'll ask Sergeant Singer if I can take you down to your bedwoom.'

'No! Not there—not yet.' I met her eyes. Suddenly we were both sharply aware of what was going on downstairs. We knew too much about the procedures following on sudden violent death.

'Oh, wight! Come upstairs, then. You can use my woom—'

'Thanks, but I'm OK. I'd rather stay around where there are other people.' Besides, it would be easier to sneak down one flight of stairs than two.

'Oh, Twixie! You don't think you're in danger? You—' Her eyes widened even more. 'You didn't *see* anything—anyone—you could identify? Someone who might want to get wid of you?'

'No, no, nothing like that. I didn't see a thing.' I only wished I had.

'Yes, but suppose someone watching outside *thought* you'd seen him?' Des chimed in.

The idea was disquieting. Who could tell what a killer, who must be in a state of high nervous tension, might think? I had turned to face the window just after the arrow crashed through it—and the archer must have felt hellishly conspicuous, wielding the great bow.

'You're a real Job's comforter,' I told Des.

'Huh?' Job looked up. 'What was that? Somebody taking my name in vain?'

'That would be impossible. Anyway, we were talking about the other Job—the Biblical one.'

'Him?' Job snorted. 'He didn't know what troubles were. He shoulda been in my shoes. I've got problems he never even thought of. I tell you, Trixie, I'm a charter member of the If-I'd-known-I-was-going-to-last-this-long, I'd-have-taken-better-care-of-myself-Club.'

'Of course, some people make their own troubles.' Griselda's voice throbbed with many meanings. The veiled look she sent Job made him squirm.

'This woman—' Griselda addressed me abruptly. 'You say that she was imitating me when she was killed?'

'That's right. She was draping herself all over the doorway, the way you do.' I was too tired to be tactful.

'Ja, they all mimic me like that.' She shrugged. 'It is good publicity. Even the drag acts.'

Especially the drag acts. Griselda had long since become one of their over-the-top cult heroines.

'She was awfully good.' I felt impelled to defend Cressida. 'Even without the right wig and make-up, it would have been hard to tell you apart—from a distance.'

'So—' Griselda glanced obliquely at Job. 'And there are many people who do not wish me to publish my memoirs. Too many secrets repose in my breast. I know, as you say, where too many bodies are buried.'

'Now wait a minute—' Job protested.

'Yes—' Griselda silenced him with another look. 'It

would be most convenient for many people if their secrets were to die with me.'

That was what I had been thinking, but as soon as Griselda voiced it, I began to think again. She was too quick to take the role of menaced heroine for herself. Not many people who knew her would be worried about those threatened memoirs—they had been threatening for too many years, and had always been averted by the right pay-off. Only a bankrupt would face any danger from Griselda.

Suddenly, I wondered just how healthy Job's finances really were. Not too bad, surely, if he was mounting a stage musical and also considering a new film. On the other hand, all this activity might have left him perilously overcommitted.

'Sweetheart—' Job laid his hand over his heart. 'I'd never do anything to hurt you. Just like you'd never do anything to hurt me—even if you knew anything worth knowing, which you couldn't, because there isn't anything to know.'

'Really?' Griselda raised one eyebrow. 'What about—?'

I took a sudden coughing fit. I might have overdone it. It sounded more like whooping cough than your ordinary tickle in the throat, but it stopped them dead. The room was quiet as I tried to cope with a cough that had suddenly taken on a life of its own.

'You were saying—?' Sergeant Singer prompted as I wheezed into silence. He looked at Griselda hopefully.

'Saying?' Griselda gave him a puzzled frown. Sparring with Job was an occupational hazard, but our private quarrels were no business of outsiders. Especially policemen.

'Oh yes.' Her face cleared. 'I was saying that Trixie has a nasty cough. She should take something for it.'

'Good idea!' I was grateful to her for the cue.

'I'll get you a glass of water.' Des started for the door.

'I'll get my own!' I sent him a look that stopped him dead in his tracks.

Gwenda helped me to my feet and showed every indication of coming with me. She was of sterner stuff than Des and my glare bounced off her.

'Thank you, dear—' I shook off her hand. 'I can manage. Besides—' I smiled sweetly. 'I want to use the bathroom.' It was the one excuse no one could argue with—and it ensured complete privacy.

They watched me leave with varying degrees of suspicion, particularly Sergeant Singer. I gave him an extra-sweet smile as I closed the door behind me. He gave me an old-fashioned look, but there was nothing he could do.

Both the upper and lower hallways were deserted. A chill lingered in the ground-floor hall, as though the front door had stood open for a time while policemen came and went, carrying out their equipment—and their sad burden. I shivered, as I slipped the key into the Yale lock and opened Martha's door.

The children were motionless in the big bed. At some time, Martha must have stolen in to check on them. The curtains were drawn and a comforting night light had been rigged up in one corner of the room. Two mugs were on the bedside table and a plate with cookie crumbs. She must have brought them a snack, too. I began to feel a bit better.

'Is everything all right?' Martha was suddenly behind me.

'Where did you come from?' I hadn't heard her approach.

'I needed to be alone for a while.' We moved into the room and closed the door behind us, speaking softly. 'The police wanted to interview Hugh as . . . as next-of-kin . . . and I came downstairs. I didn't want to see anyone . . . or speak to anyone . . . so I've been sitting in the conservatory in the dark . . . thinking.'

I patted her shoulder. With all she'd had to think about,

she'd still found time to come and see that the children were comfortable.

'I'm sorry she's dead, of course, but it *is* going to make things easier for Hugh . . . and me. Oh, Mother—' her voice quavered—'life is so complicated!'

'It always was, dear.' Especially for my poor Martha, who faced the world so intensely. Only recently, with Hugh, had she begun to relax and enjoy life more. And now this had happened.

We both sighed, each following our own line of thought. And there was a further complication. Perhaps, while we were confessing, I should take my turn.

'Martha, the children—'

'It's all right, Mother, I know. Hugh told me. I'm glad he did. He also said—and I think he's right—that it would be best to let the police think that I knew it all along. Otherwise . . . it's even more complicated.' She sighed again. 'He pointed out that you can't just take children in as though they were stray kittens. The Law would have something to say about that—and they're already going to say enough.'

'I suppose so.' We had learned that they usually did. It was unfortunate that this had had to happen so soon upon the heels of our last unhappy involvement with the law. We had not endeared ourselves to Superintendent Heyhoe then and he showed no signs of having learned to love us in the meantime.

'Anyway—' Martha looked from the night light to the empty mugs. 'It was sweet of you to come and see to them.'

'I didn't,' I said. 'I thought you did. I just this minute got here and found the room like this and the little darlings dead to the world—'

'Dead . . .?' Martha echoed. We looked at each other in sudden panic and raced over to the bedside. Martha bent over them anxiously.

'Are they all right?' I had to back up as she straightened abruptly, eyes flashing.

'Please, Mother, breathe the other way for a minute. I want to check something—' She picked up one of the mugs and sniffed at it.

'I'm not—'

'No, but they are!' She thrust the mug under my nose. 'Smell that! Those dregs are loaded with brandy. The children aren't asleep—they're in a drunken stupor!'

'Oh no! But I don't understand. Who could—?' I broke off as we looked at each other in a surmise that was not so wild.

'Evangeline!'

'Can I help it if the kids can't hold their liquor?' Evangeline drawled in a highly reminiscent manner.

'Evangeline, how could you?' I should have known it. The only time she had ever approved of W. C. Fields had been when he spiked Baby Leroy's orange juice with gin from his private supply. And that had been what he'd said, too, when the poor infant had gone down for the count: 'The kid can't hold his liquor.'

'Miss Sinclair, you've gone too far!' Martha was pale and shaking with fury. 'How dare you give those poor children brandy?'

'Well, there wasn't any paregoric in the house,' Evangeline said, in a tone of sweet reasonableness. 'And it worked, didn't it?'

'Oh, Mother!' Martha turned to me. 'Tell her— Tell her—'

'They were awake,' Evangeline said. 'I found them peeking round the door. Would you rather have had them running around the house and finding their—the body?'

So Evangeline had also identified the children. I suppose

that wasn't surprising. She had said that she remembered
Cressida as a child—and there must be a strong family
resemblance to Sir Garrick.

'I don't know what Hugh will say—'

'If you're going to start your marriage by running to
tell him every least little thing,' Evangeline said tartly, 'I
wouldn't give it much chance of success.'

'Evangeline—'

'Mother—'

'Hhrph-hrrph!' The sound from the doorway, immediately followed by a loud knock, made us all jump.

The young constable was standing there. We had left the
door open when we rushed in to confront Evangeline. Now
I wondered uneasily how long he had been standing there
and how much he had heard.

Still, we hadn't broken any law. Or had we?

'Pardon me—' If we had, he wasn't going to bother about
it; the police had enough on their plate as it was. 'But
Superintendent Heyhoe would like to speak to you now,
Miss Dolan.'

'Oh yes . . .' I started towards him.

'Not you, madam.' He stopped me. '*That* Miss Dolan.'
He pointed to Martha.

CHAPTER 15

'There goes the ball game!' Evangeline crossed to the doorway and looked after them. 'Pity I couldn't have doped her
along with the children. That Superintendent Whey-Hoo
will tie her in knots. Once she opens her mouth and starts
talking, she'll incriminate herself with every word.'

'Oh, I hope not.' But I was afraid Evangeline was right.
Martha had always been too honest for her own good, which

meant she wasn't very tactful, either. She would be no match for Superintendent Heyhoe.

'Trixie!' Evangeline stared at me as though she had just realized I was there. 'Where's Griselda?'

'In the upstairs sitting-room.'

'Where's Job? Where's Julian?'

'In the upstairs sitting-room.'

'You left them *alone* up there? With *Grisly?*' Evangeline started down the hallway. 'Are you out of your mind?'

'Gwenda and Des are there, too.' I hurried after her, barely able to keep up. She could put on amazing bursts of speed when her best interests were concerned. She was taking the stairs at a pace that would have put the kids to shame.

A wave of her hand dismissed Gwenda and Des. I wished she'd keep hold of the stair rail when she was running like that. Suppose she tripped?

'Grisly will eat them for breakfast!' She didn't mean Gwenda and Des.

And Evangeline already had them marked down for her own menu.

At the top of the stairs she whirled and swooped down the corridor with renewed speed. She couldn't have done it faster on a broomstick. I struggled along behind her, trying to keep from panting.

Evangeline paused at the door, not to give me a chance to catch up, but to listen for a moment and draw herself up to her full height before flinging open the door. The old subtitle '*AHA!*' seemed to float silently across her back.

'*Too late!*' floated above Griselda's head. She lounged back in her chair with the air of a cat who had just finished licking the last drop of cream from her chops. Sergeant Julian Singer knelt at one side of her chair, gazing up at her raptly. Job, obviously realizing that if he got that far down he'd never get up again, contented himself with hanging over the back of her chair, beaming down at her fondly.

'Here they are!' Job transferred his beam to us. 'Now we can get everything settled, nice and easy.' Cream was dripping from his whiskers, as well.

'Settle what?' Evangeline slid into the room like a glacier; the temperature dropped twenty degrees.

I hurriedly closed the door behind us, feeling that it wouldn't do Sergeant Singer's police career any good if Superintendent Heyhoe should catch him on his knees in the midst of a group of suspects. It might even lead to nasty questions about a conflict of interests.

'The film, of course. The film!' Job said. 'What have we been talking about all night?'

Well, the rest of us had spared an occasional word for the murder in our midst, but you don't get to be Director without a strong element of monomania in your make-up.

'I am delighted to be able to tell you—' Job spoke as though addressing a Press Conference. 'Griselda von Kirstenberg has agreed to be the star of my picture! *One* of the stars,' he amended quickly.

'*She's* in the picture?' Evangeline's voice rose incredulously.

'I have told you, Job—' Griselda did not like either the emendation or the incredulity. 'I could play a double role, even triple. With the split screen, it would be no problem. And it would be a *tour de force*.'

'Yes, yes.' Job patted her shoulder absently. 'But it will be even better with all of you in it. Think of it—three living legends in the same film. *My* film. *That* would be a real *tour de force*.'

'I could do it,' Griselda brooded. 'I would be magnificent!'

'You would *all* be magnificent!' Job was selling the idea for all he was worth. 'Three stars who will never cease to shine, appearing together—to show the world what film acting is all about!'

'I could do it all. I can do anything Evangeline can do—' Griselda straightened in her chair, assuming an air of hauteur. 'And better.'

'Anyone could imitate you!' Evangeline's eyes glinted dangerously. 'Not that anyone would want to right now. Unfortunately, you appear to have a short-sighted enemy.'

'You are wrong! No one would wish to kill me. I am universally beloved. My fanmail filled three filing cabinets last year alone. Four-drawer filing cabinets!'

'Girls, girls—' Job called them to order in the old way. 'Let us keep our eyes upon the doughnut and not upon the hole. We are discussing my next film and your appearance in it.

'Evangeline, my angel! Trixie, my love! Say you'll do it!'

'I don't know . . .' Evangeline went coy; it was a frightening sight.

'My sweethearts—only you can do it. Together, we shall all create our Autumn Masterpiece!'

Evangeline didn't care for that 'autumn' although, in her case, 'winter' might have been more accurate. Her face froze.

'On my knees, I would beg you—if I could get down there. Young man—you're already on your knees. Persuade her!'

'Evangeline—' Obligingly, Sergeant Singer shuffled towards her, still on his knees. 'Please say you will. You don't know how wonderful it could be. I have some leave coming. We can continue to work on your autobiography and—' His face shone. 'And I can write a book about the making of the film at the same time. Mr Farraday promised me—'

'Maybe even additional dialogue,' Job said indulgently.

'We'll see how it goes. You'll be right there on the spot and it would do you good to get a line in the credits.'

'You see?' Sergeant Singer's face was alight with bliss, a whole new career was opening out before him. Or maybe he was just counting his chickens before they were hatched.

I felt a cold chill of foreboding. The Police Department paid a salary, steady, regular and with foreseeable improvements at stated intervals. It was better than anything Job could offer. Additional dialogue, indeed!

'Oh, all right.' Evangeline capitulated. 'I suppose it can't do any harm.'

It certainly couldn't be worse than *Queen Leah*. But that icy feeling at the nape of my neck persisted.

'Shouldn't we see the script first?' I tried to sound a note of caution.

'You see, Job? She is not truly interested,' Griselda said. 'It does not matter. I can play her role. It will be easy—' She rearranged her features into a vapid simper. 'Und I will wear low shoes. No one could tell the difference.'

'I'll do it!' I snapped. I met Evangeline's eyes and we pantomimed a spit on the palm of our hands and started towards each other, hands outstretched. We'd act that German sausage right off the screen.

Before our hands could connect, Sergeant Singer had seized them both and was kissing them. That was all very well, but it did not dispel the growing chill that, strangely, still seemed to be centred on the back of my neck. Uneasily, I began to identify it as a persistent draught.

Just as I made the identification, while Sergeant Singer was still bowed in homage over our hands—and still on his knees—there was an ominous sound behind us.

Someone cleared his throat menacingly in the doorway.

I didn't need to turn around to see who was standing there. The stricken look on Julian Singer's face told me.

'SERGEANT SINGER!'

In slow motion, Sergeant Singer dropped our hands and surged to his feet. The blood drained from his face. His mouth opened and closed silently a few times. There wasn't much he could say.

'Sometimes, Singer,' Superintendent Heyhoe spoke with deceptive mildness, although his face was choleric, 'just occasionally, I get the impression that your heart isn't in police work.'

'Y-yes, sir— N-no, sir—' Singer stuttered. 'I m-mean—'

'I wouldn't want to interfere with your little sideline as a gigolo, but I *would* like a word with you. If you're not too busy, that is.'

'Sir!' Sergeant Singer snapped to attention, rigid and unmoving.

'Not here, Sergeant. *You* may have no secrets from your . . . friends, but I have. Step outside!'

'Sir!' Still at attention, Sergeant Singer moved robot-like to follow his superior into the hall. The door slammed behind him.

'I'm afraid that young man is in trouble,' Job said.

He wasn't the only one. Abruptly, I realized that Evangeline and I had committed ourselves sight unseen to Job's next movie. Just because Griselda had antagonized us. It wasn't a very good reason.

'It does not matter.' Griselda shrugged. 'If he loses his job, then he will have more time to devote to us.'

'To *me*, you mean.' Evangeline glared at her. 'I have first call on Julian's services.'

'And Hugh has first call on *our* services,' I reminded everyone. It might be our salvation. If Hugh could mount that production of *Arsenic and Old Lace* before Job got rolling . . . 'Where *is* Hugh?' I wanted to light a fire under him.

'He put his head wound the door a little while ago—' Gwenda and Des emerged from the corner where they had taken cover, like proper little juvenile leads, while the main action went on centre-stage. 'I think he was looking for Martha, but she wasn't here so he went away again. He didn't say anything, but he looked wather stwange.'

'So would you—after the third degree,' Evangeline said knowledgeably.

'No, honestly,' Des protested. 'We don't do things like that in this country.'

'I'm sure you believe that, but you weren't put through what I had to go through the last time. They might not have used physical force, but—oh!—the mental cruelty!'

'You are using the language of a divorce petition,' Griselda observed dispassionately. 'But then, you have issued so many, it undoubtedly comes more naturally to you.'

'We don't have the Third Degree in the States any more, either,' I intervened quickly. 'There are all sorts of rules and regulations. That sort of thing went on in the 'thirties —not now.'

'She is living in the past. It is a bad sign. Can she remember her lines?'

'No, Evangeline.' I caught her arm as she started for Griselda. 'You can't assault her here—there are too many witnesses.'

'You're right. I'll get her later.'

'Girls, girls!' Job was not entirely displeased. 'Save it until the cameras are turning. Don't waste it.'

'I'm afraid there's plenty more where that came from.' And I was afraid Job was going to egg them on once he got them on the set together. It was just his style. That and slave-driving. How could we get ourselves out of this commitment?

I had to find Hugh. He couldn't have gone far, not while the children were still here. Perhaps he was downstairs with them. Oh dear—that thought brought no comfort. What if he had discovered they had been drugged with brandy?

He'd never allow them in the house again. It was no way to start out a step-grandmotherly relationship. I sighed. Life was never simple—not with Evangeline around.

'That's better,' Job said. Evangeline and Griselda had subsided into ritualized sneers and head-tossings. 'We've done well tonight and there are great things in store. Tell you what —why don't I telephone the theatre and leave a message for Posy and the gang to come round after the performance? She'll be designing your costumes and she can take some preliminary measurements. Where's the telephone?'

'In the study,' Gwenda said, 'but the police are there. P'waps you'd wather use the extension in Jasper's bedwoom?'

'Yeah, that might be a better idea.' Job looked around. 'Where is it?'

'I'll show you—' Remembering Job's reputation with young girls, I forestalled Gwenda's offer. Also, I could slip away from there while Job was telephoning and look for Hugh.

We started towards Jasper's room, but never reached it. The door burst open suddenly and Martha rushed into the room and flung herself upon me.

'Oh, Mother!' she sobbed. 'Oh, Mother—they're taking me to the police station. They—they told me to pack a bag!'

'I hate to admit it,' Evangeline said, 'but I can see Hee-Haw's point. Martha is seething with motive, means and opportunity. I'd have arrested her myself.'

'She has not been arrested,' I said between clenched teeth. 'She is merely helping the police with their inquiries.'

'Same difference.' Evangeline brought me a glass of brandy. We had retreated to her bedroom downstairs to lick our wounds while Martha packed, Job telephoned and Griselda took her turn at being questioned.

'And she had no opportunity—' I didn't feel strong

enough to dispute the other two points. 'She was with Hugh every minute.'

'Hah! No country in the world allows a married couple to alibi each other—and they're as good as. Hugh's testimony is worthless.'

'Just shut up, Evangeline! I'm trying to think.'

'Quite right. We have a great deal of thinking to do. What does one wear for the Old Bailey, I wonder? Perhaps a variation of the costume I had when I was touring the Straw Hat Circuit with *The Trial of Mary Dugan* . . .'

'Evangeline! It is not going to come to a trial. Martha is innocent!'

'Of course she is. She hasn't the gumption to kill anyone. But that won't stop the cops from railroading her.'

It was no use, she had played in too many gangster movies in their heyday. So had I. Nightmare visions crowded my mind: a cell block, steel bars, cages ranged around a circular area open to the roof—except for the wire-mesh safety net, so that any prisoner leaping over an upper railing would be caught before hitting the cement floor. And Martha, my athletic California girl, locked in one of those claustrophobic narrow cells—

'Not black. That would be defeatist. It would look as though we were expecting the worst.'

'Evangeline—*please!*'

'Navy, perhaps, or dove grey, with touches of crisp white close to the face—'

'Evangeline, I'm warning you—' But she'd snapped me out of the nightmare mood. Sheer annoyance had set my brain functioning again.

Martha hadn't done it, that was the one certainty in my Universe. The trouble was that someone had. Who?

Trevor had the means—he'd been taking archery lessons all day. He might also have had the opportunity, if he had been lying about the time he was supposed to report for duty at the Harpo. But . . . the motive? I sketched a brief scenario in which he was Cressida's discarded Toy Boy taking revenge for being cast aside, but I couldn't convince myself.

Hugh was far more likely. I had been trying not to think that, but once the thought crept into my mind, it would not be dislodged.

Hugh had more motive than anyone. Cressida had been bleeding him white to support not only her and the children, but her crackpot film unit as well. She had been emotionally blackmailing him with the constant threat of withdrawing access to the children. The last straw could have been when he realized that, having lost the children, she was callously prepared to capitalize on it with that phoney ransom demand. Not only motive, but provocation. And, without Cressida around, his relationship with Martha would run a lot more smoothly.

The more I thought about it, the more surprised I was that Superintendent Heyhoe was concentrating on Martha. Or was that just a ploy to force Hugh into a confession? Wearily, I took another sip of brandy.

'Yes,' Evangeline spoke as though she had been following my thoughts, but her next words proved she hadn't. 'It must have been a nasty shock for Job when he discovered he'd killed the wrong woman.'

'You really think Griselda was meant to be the victim?' The thought cheered me immediately.

'She's been asking for it for years. Decades! And she'll get it yet.' Evangeline's eyes gleamed. 'I shouldn't be at all surprised if that isn't isn't why Job was so anxious to get her in his new picture. He wants to have another try at her.'

'Evangeline!' I looked over my shoulder nervously. 'If anyone should hear you . . .'

'Tell the truth and shame the devil.' Evangeline blithely overlooked the fact that her version of the truth rarely resembled anyone else's. But this time she had a good case. Except possibly against Job.

'Maybe Superintendent Heyhoe would stop picking on Martha,' I said wistfully, 'if only we could persuade him that the arrow was meant for Griselda.'

'By now, he must be convinced of it.' Evangeline consulted her watch. 'He's had Grisly all to himself for the past twenty minutes. That should do it.'

'I think you may be right.' Hope began to stir in me. Superintendent Heyhoe had little patience with giant egos —and Griselda's was even more gigantic than Evangeline's.

'Of course I am. You may have noticed that Ho-Ho has a short fuse. We can safely depend on Grisly to light it.'

'She does have a gift for antagonizing everyone.'

'If I weren't around, she'd be her own worst enemy.' Evangeline topped up her glass and came over to refill mine.

'I'm not sure I ought—'

'Nonsense!' She splashed brandy into my glass. 'We've got to have something to keep us going—and food seems to be in short supply around here lately.'

'That's right.' Now that she mentioned it, I realized that I was starving. 'We've missed dinner.'

'Not to mention tea and supper. It's coming up to midnight snack time—so drink up. It will do you good.'

'Some food would do us better. Come on.' I got up and headed for the kitchen. 'There must be something we can rustle up.' I felt guilty for thinking about food when my daughter was about to be whisked away to the police station, but my stomach overruled my head. Besides, we would be of no use to Martha if we collapsed.

'Now you're talking!' Evangeline was right beside me as we walked into the dark kitchen and snapped on the light.

'Oh!' I gave a gasp of horror.

Hugh was sitting bolt upright on one of the kitchen chairs, his eyes glazed and unseeing.

CHAPTER 16

'What?' He blinked in the sudden brightness and came back to life. 'Trixie—' He pushed back his chair and rushed over to me, grabbing me by my upper arms in a grip that made me wince. 'Trixie, Martha didn't do it!'

'Of course she didn't,' I said soothingly. I could not bring myself to ask: *Did you?*

'What are you doing sitting here in the dark?' Evangeline asked.

'I wanted to think.'

'What's the matter—was the conservatory occupied?'

'As a matter of fact, it was—is. Cres—' His voice broke, he tried again. 'Cressida's crazy friends are in there. I heard them whispering, so I came in here.'

'Are they still here? I thought the police had got rid of them.' Now that there was no prospect of *Queen Leah* going ahead, Evangeline had no time or patience to spare for her erstwhile colleagues. *That* little flutter with Art and Feminist Statements hadn't lasted long.

'They're very upset.' Hugh seemed to feel obscurely moved to defend them. 'They thought a lot of Cressida.'

'Dear boy, we all did.' Evangeline remembered just in time that Cressida had almost been her employer—and Hugh was still about to be. 'This is utterly shattering for everyone concerned. And in *our* house, too!'

'I'm sorry.' Hugh was back on familiar ground apologizing; his grip on me relaxed and I took the opportunity to move back out of his reach. 'I wouldn't have had this happen for the world.'

'It's not—' Evangeline stopped short of assuring him that it wasn't his fault and settled for: 'These things happen.'

'Especially when you're around, eh, Miss Sinclair?' Superintendent Heyhoe stood in the doorway looking at his old adversary speculatively.

'Haven't you anything better to do, Hi-Yo, than sneak around eavesdropping in doorways?' Evangeline was ready to meet him head-on.

'As a matter of fact, madam—' Heyhoe matched her sneer for sneer—'I have a murder case to solve. And now that I've had the opportunity to interview Miss Von Kirstenberg, it appears that it may also be a particularly nasty case of mistaken identity. I'm ready to hear your view of the matter now, madam.'

I knew it! Once Grisly began shooting her mouth off, no policeman in his right mind could fail to spot the fact that she would have been the ideal victim. And, no doubt at all, she would have helped his deductive processes by pointing out how thoroughly Evangeline detested her.

Evangeline, of course, had already decided that Job was the killer and, as she would point out, he had the track record on fatal accidents to prove it. Depending on how thoroughly Heyhoe annoyed her in the impending interview, she would either withhold this theory or blurt it out. All looked dark, but then I glimpsed the silver lining.

'Can Martha stop packing now?'

'Packing?' Hugh was instantly alert. 'Why is Martha packing?'

'Superintendent Heyhoe was going to take her down to police headquarters, but of course he can't do that now.'

'Why?' Heyhoe had forgotten I was there, ready to attack his flank. He swung to face me, snarling.

'Well,' I explained reasonably, 'if you're not even sure who the victim was supposed to be, you can't arrest someone with a motive—an alleged motive—for killing Cressida, when it was really someone with a motive for doing away with Griselda, who just happened to get the wrong person.'

'Nice one.' Evangeline nodded approval. Even her dizzy *Happy Couple* bride had never made so rambling and convoluted a stab at a solution. Superintendent Heyhoe was looking dazed.

'That's right,' Hugh seconded me. 'You've got to let Martha go.'

'No one—' Heyhoe siezed on the one firm point for rebuttal in my statement—'no one is under arrest—yet. Miss Dolan is merely going to help the police with their inquiries.

'Help them waste their time, you mean!' Evangeline snapped. 'If, as any fool would know, Grisly was the real target, then you should be looking for someone who could cop a plea of justifiable homicide—and not bothering poor Martha. And if—'

'Stop iffing about!' Heyhoe thundered. 'I mean—' he pulled himself together with a visible effort. 'I mean, I wish to speak to you, Miss Sinclair. I mean, I'd appreciate your help—'

'Shall I pack a bag?' Evangeline widened her eyes in exaggerated innocence.

'That won't be necessary, madam.' Heyhoe could not control a massive shudder. 'There are just a few questions—'

'You can't have it both ways,' I said. He looked as though he would like to try. 'You can't take Martha away to help with your inquiries and let Evangeline stay here while *she* helps.'

'Thank you, Trixie,' Evangeline murmured. 'It's such a comfort to know I can always depend on you—to railroad me.'

'Nothing of the sort—' Heyhoe began.

'There better not be!' I cut him off. 'It's been quiet so far because it's Saturday night, almost—' I glanced at my watch—'Sunday morning. The Press and media haven't got hold of this yet. But you can't keep them out of it much longer. They'll be around here howling for their Monday morning headlines. We'll have to speak to them, of course—'

He gave me a nasty look, catching on at once. Fortunately for us, and unfortunately for him, Evangeline and I had become the darlings of the media since our arrival in London. They were uncompromisingly on our side and against anyone who might upset us.

'If you take Martha away, I'll be so upset—' I let my lower lip wobble and caught it between my teeth in the Gallant Little Chorine mannerism that had stood me so well in all those musicals when I was passed over for the leading role because the Director wanted it for his girlfriend. 'I'll be so upset, I just don't know *what* I might say.'

'And I—' Evangeline chimed in—'might even weep.' That was a serious threat. Evangeline's tears had been one of the wonders of Hollywood; she could turn them on at the drop of a hanky—and without the aid of glycerine. She could still do it. She stared off into middle distance with a look of noble suffering while the tears gathered in her eyes as they had done when the wagon train moved on westwards and she looked back over her shoulder at the tiny grave on the prairie where her baby was lying.

Superintendent Heyhoe looked trapped—and furious. Some day we were going to go too far. But not today.

'All right.' Abruptly, he caved in. 'We won't need Miss Dolan at the station tonight. Not until we've carried out a few more inquiries. But,' he added hastily, 'she needn't bother to unpack yet. And I'll want a more detailed statement from *you*—' he glared at me—'as soon as I've finished with Miss Sinclair.'

'Any time,' I said. 'I'll be around.'

'Quite. Now—' he turned to Evangeline—'if you'll just come up to the study . . .'

'Up all those stairs?' Before our very eyes, Evangeline turned weak and frail. 'Again?'

'It's late,' Hugh said. 'She's exhausted. Can't this wait until morning?'

'This won't take long, sir. It's always best to get it over with while events are still fresh in the mind. Perhaps we could talk in your room, madam?'

'Certainly not!' Evangeline drew herself up, eyes flashing. Had Griselda been spreading that canard about her memory to the police? 'I have no intention of entertaining you in my bedroom, Heyday!'

Superintendent Heyhoe went through several colours of the rainbow before settling down to a startling puce. I thought he was going to have a seizure then and there.

'There is a perfectly adequate living-room on this floor,' Evangeline said, while he was still making gurgling noises. 'We can talk in there.'

'If you insist, madam.' I didn't trust the unpleasant gleam in Heyhoe's eyes. 'But I'll thank you to remember that it was your idea.'

I didn't like the sound of that and neither did Evangeline, but it *was* her idea and she couldn't back down now. She swept out in front of Heyhoe, leading the way through my room towards the living-room.

'I've been trying to reach my lawyer.' Hugh looked after them unhappily. 'I've left messages on his Ansaphone, but if he's away for the weekend, he might not respond until late tomorrow night—or perhaps Monday morning.'

'Tomorrow is practically here.' I spoke from the stomach as well as the heart. We'd come out here to see about food. I crossed to the fridge and looked inside. My thoughts had been veering towards scrambled eggs, but heaven knew how long Heyhoe would keep Evangeline tied up and they'd taste terrible cold.

Hard-boiled then, and there was a large jar of mayonnaise in there, too. I'd make egg salad sandwich filling and it wouldn't matter how long Heyhoe lingered over the questioning. I filled a saucepan with water, put half a dozen eggs into it, and set it over a medium flame where it could boil merrily for quite a while without doing any harm. Meanwhile, I could go about some other business.

'Come on,' I said to Hugh. 'Let's go and tell Martha she can stop packing.'

'You're right.' Hugh didn't need urging. His face lit up; he whirled about and charged down the hallway, abandoning Evangeline to her fate with Heyhoe.

I followed more slowly and caught up with him as he tapped softly on the door to Martha's room.

'Shhh . . .' She opened the door, finger to her lips. 'Don't wake the children.' Then she saw who it was. 'Oh, Hugh!' She fell into his arms.

'It's all right, dearest.' He caught her up and lifted her back across the threshold while she buried her face in his shoulder.

I felt a tiny forlorn pang. As a small child, she had clung to me like that. But I was happy for her and I mustn't be selfish. Perhaps I ought to tiptoe away and leave them alone.

But I wanted to make sure that the children were all right. I slipped into the room and closed the door softly behind me.

A suitcase lay open across the armchair, half-filled. Garments were strewn over the back of the chair, the wardrobe door hung ajar and a drawer gaped open. Martha had been trying to pack by the dim glow of the night light.

Hugh carried Martha to the far corner of the room murmuring endearments. It seemed to me that something more practical ought to be mentioned.

'The heat's off, Martha.' I kept my voice low, although I noticed that the children were already stirring.

'What?' Martha partially disentangled herself and raised her head.

'Superintendent Heyhoe has just interviewed Griselda. It made him realize that there's a good chance *she* was intended to be the murderee. He says you can stop packing. He's got a lot more interviewing to do before he can start carting anybody down to the station.'

'Thank heavens!' Martha's eyes began to shine.

'Evangeline is with Heyhoe now. She'll carry on with the good work.' In fact, by the time Evangeline was through filling him in on Griselda's chequered past, he would be sure he was in the presence of his Number One suspect. What a letdown it would be for him when he discovered that Evangeline was with Griselda at the time of the killing —her alibi was the intended victim herself.

'She will, won't she?' Hugh almost smiled. 'Poor Heyhoe, this must be his worst nightmare sprung to life. He'd hoped he'd seen the last of Evangeline, of all of us.'

'Hello, Daddy.' Hearing his voice, Orrie sat up in bed, yawning. 'Have you come to take us home?'

'You're awake, are you?' Hugh and Martha sprang apart. From what I could see, they needn't have bothered. The children had already noticed with interest, but no displeasure, that they had been entwined in each other's arms.

'Darlings, how do you feel!' Martha hurried over to them anxiously. 'You don't have headaches, do you?'

'It's my stomach, not my head,' Orrie said. 'I'm hungry.'

'So am I,' Vi agreed.

'The eggs!' I had left them to boil in the kitchen; they must be done by now. 'I can have some nice egg salad sandwiches for you in just a few minutes. And some more cocoa.'

'The cocoa tasted funny.' Orrie wrinkled his nose. 'Could we have some tea, please?'

'Of course you can.'

'What's egg salad?' Vi was suspicious.

'Egg mayonnaise,' Martha translated. She was adapting fast.

'Oh, that's all right.' Vi's face cleared.

'*Are* you taking us home, Daddy?' Orrie refused to stay sidetracked.

'Yes,' Hugh said. 'That is—' His mouth worked as he tried to find words to tell the children what had happened. 'That is, not right away. But eventually, yes. Your . . . your mother has had an accident, so we'll have to hang about here for a bit. Why don't you try to go back to sleep?'

'I'm not tired any more.' Orrie was on the alert, sensing more than he had been told. 'What happened to Mummy? Mum?'

'I'll go and see to those sandwiches.' I backed towards the door. This was one scene Hugh had to handle for himself and an audience wouldn't help.

'I'll come with you, Mother.'

'Please, Martha—' Hugh's voice was unsteady. 'Stay here.'

'Martha—' Vi's lips trembled, she was on the verge of tears, overwhelmed by the atmosphere, by the feeling of something unknown waiting to engulf her. 'I want Martha!'

'Please, Martha,' Hugh said again.

'Martha-a-a . . .' Vi wailed.

Martha went to her. Orrie squirmed over to be included in the embrace. Hugh sat down beside Martha on the edge of the bed and put his arms around them all.

'Where's Mummy?' Orrie asked. 'Is she in hospital?' It was the worst he could imagine.

I backed out silently and closed the door behind me.

Gwenda and Des were tiptoeing down the stairs, looking frightened.

'Twixie—where have all the police gone? We need them now. Des and I just looked out of the upstairs window and, and—there's someone prowling awound outside!'

CHAPTER 17

'That's all we need!' I leaned against the wall and tried to gather my thoughts to deal with this new emergency. 'Isn't Sergeant Singer upstairs?'

'We looked,' Des said, 'but we couldn't find him.'

'We couldn't find anyone. Evwyone's disappeared!'

'Superintendent Heyhoe is in the living-room with Evangeline.' Even making allowances for Gwenda's taste for the dramatic, it did not seem possible that the house was suddenly deserted. 'Hugh and Martha are in with the children . . . breaking the news.'

'Oh, how tewwible! Is there anything I can do?'

'Nova and Lucy are in the conservatory.' I shook my head to Gwenda's offer and continued my round-up. 'And I thought Griselda and Job were upstairs with you.'

'They were, but they left,' Des said. 'We thought they'd come down here.'

'Maybe they've stepped outside for a breath of air.' It wasn't much, but it was the best I could suggest on the spur of the moment. 'They might be the ones you saw from the window.'

'We know *them*,' Gwenda said scornfully. 'These were stwangers and—and there was an air of *menace* about them!'

I took a deep breath. I hadn't really believed that explanation myself. Neither Grisly nor Job were the 'breath of air' type; a quick trip down to the nearest pub was more their style. Except that all the pubs had closed by this time.

'If Superintendent Heyhoe is the only policeman awound, shouldn't we tell *him* about the pwowlers?' Gwenda was still playing her scene to the hilt.

'He shouldn't be the only policeman around,' I said. 'There ought to be one or two on guard outside. We can report to Heyhoe, but if his guards have left their posts, he isn't going to like it.'

'You're wight, he'll be fuwious. P'waps we ought to just take a quick look outside ourselves first, to make sure.'

'I don't think that's a good idea, dear.' I felt quite faint at the thought of opening the front door and standing at the top of the steps with the light behind us silhouetting us as targets for whatever might be prowling through the grounds.

'Oh, come on, Twixie. There are thwee of us.' Gwenda was ready for combat.

'You stay here, Trixie.' Des was more practical, if less flattering. 'We'll go.'

'Wait a minute.' I didn't want them racing outside and risking their necks. If the intruder had murderous intent and had missed his correct target the first time, he might be back—and armed with a more modern weapon—to try again. And he might have begun by knocking off those guards.

'Des, run upstairs and take another look around for Sergeant Singer. Please. He can't have gone far and it will be better if we have someone official with us if we go hunting for intruders.'

'OK.' Des shrugged amiably and whirled around, taking the stairs two at a time.

'Gwenda, come and help me, dear.' I herded her before me as I headed for the kitchen to rescue the eggs before the pan burned dry.

'All wight.' I got the impression that she was not entirely loath to postpone her heroic scene. 'If you insist.'

'I do.' I turned off the gas, noting with relief that there was still half an inch of bubbling water in the saucepan. 'Get me a large bowl from the cupboard, please. And the jar of mayonnaise from the fridge.'

'Wight!' She carried out her allotted tasks with such enthusiasm that I suspected that she was ready for a midnight snack herself.

I was running cold water over the eggs when I became aware of odd noises in the distance. At first, I thought Gwenda was having trouble juggling bowl and jar, but when I turned around, I saw that she had set them both down on the table and was looking off in the direction of my room. The clinking noises continued.

'The conservatory—' I started for it. 'They may be trying to break in.' I'd never liked the idea of living in a glass house, and having a glass extension to my room fell into the same category.

'Don't wowwy, Twixie—' Gwenda caught up a carving knife, really making me worry, and followed. 'We'll get them!'

I gestured her to silence and we crept up on the conservatory.

'There *must* be a key—' Nova was shaking the glass door into the garden, rattling the lock.

'There isn't,' Lucy argued. 'If I could find the light switch, you could see for yourself.'

'Allow *me*.' I flipped the switch and light flooded the small artificial room. Ferns and assorted greenery sprang into life. On the far side of this domesticated jungle, Nova and Lucy clawed at the door, standing out clearly against the blackness of the garden beyond.

'You see?' Lucy cried triumphantly. 'No key!'

Once again we were all on a brightly-lit stage. Once again, predators lurked outside.

I flipped the light switch off and the merciful darkness

enveloped us. Rain drummed on the roof panes overhead.

'My eyes!' Nova complained. 'I can't see a thing. What the hell did you do that for?'

'There's someone outside.'

'I know. That's why we're trying to get out. It must be the kids. They've come back.'

'The children are safe inside,' I said. 'They've been asleep. Hugh is with them now.'

'The kids are here?' Nova tried to take it in.

'Then who's outside?' Lucy's fearful voice rose. 'Get back—' There were scuffling noises. 'Get away from that door!'

There was a small crash as a potted plant bit the dust.

'They can't get in, can they?' Lucy's voice was a lot nearer.

'The key isn't on the outside of the lock, is it?' Nova was almost bumping into me.

'I don't think so.' Suddenly, I wasn't sure. So many people had been roaming in and out of the house all day; I couldn't tell what any of them might have done. Even the police might have been fooling around with the locks.

We stood in the darkness, the rain beating like muffled tom-toms against the glass. My eyes grew accustomed to the darkness and forms began to take shape; aspidistra and maidenhair fern seemed to sway in a wind that could not possibly reach them from outside. Ivy trailing from hanging baskets scratched against the glass.

'Look!' Lucy gave a small shriek and pointed to the door.

Two dark shapes loomed outside, white blobs of faces pressed against the glass and a sharp steady tapping began.

'They want to come in,' Gwenda wailed. 'Oh, Twixie, who—*who* are they? *What* are they?'

I knew what she was thinking. It was a night for ghosts. And there had been death in that garden before.

'Take it easy,' I said. 'It can't be them. You know it

can't.' The dead didn't return and stand swearing at you in mellifluous theatrical voices because you weren't fast enough at opening the door and letting them in. Furthermore, there was something vaguely familiar about them.

'Be careful, Twixie,' Gwenda said, as I advanced cautiously.

'Job! Trixie!' They were beating on the glass with knuckles and the flat of their palms. 'Job! Miss Dolan! Let us in!'

'Wait a minute,' I called loudly. I fished under a potted plant on the bench beside the door and found the key. I had forgotten that Job had been expecting his friends to call round after the show. I stabbed at the lock with the key and finally connected. I swung the door open and stepped back as they crowded in.

'God! What a filthy night! Only Job could expect people to come chasing after him on a night like this!'

Gwenda snapped the light on and lowered the carving knife, reassured by voices which belonged so unmistakably to colleagues.

'Leave your raincoats here,' I suggested. 'You don't want to go dripping through the house.'

'I should say not!' Clive Anderson shucked off his sodden coat and tossed it over the bench before pecking at my cheek. 'You're an angel! Heaven to see you again, my sweet.'

'Where *is* Job?' Whitby Grant blew me the obligatory kiss and draped his coat beside Clive's.

'Good question,' I said. 'We're thinking of getting up a search party. But why didn't you come in the front door?'

'We tried, but nobody seemed willing to answer the bell.' Clive scraped his shoes on the inner doormat, trying to dislodge the worst of the mud and leafmould.

'I didn't hear it,' I said.

'Neither did I.' Whitby shuffled his feet over the mat. 'It must be out of order.'

'That wouldn't surprise me.' After the workout it had had this weekend, it had probably given up the ghost.

'Who are *they*?' Nova demanded.

'Friends of friends,' I answered absently and turned back to the newcomers. 'Come into the—' I broke off the invitation. Evangeline and Superintendent Heyhoe were in the living-room. And 'Come into the bedroom' didn't have the proper ring to it.

'Come into the kitchen,' I decided. 'We're having tea and sandwiches. You can dry out.'

'Oh, we couldn't,' Clive demurred.

'I'm not hungry,' Whit said gruffly.

'I could use a sandwich,' Nova said. 'Couldn't you, Lu? I can't remember when we last ate.'

'We ate before the show,' Clive said. 'We just came by to talk to Job. We got a message from him at the theatre. He *is* still here, isn't he?'

'Your guess is as good as mine.' I turned and headed for the kitchen, hoping everyone would follow my lead.

'What do you mean?' Whit was right behind me. 'Has he left?'

'How did you get into the back garden?' I countered with a question of my own. 'There was supposed to be a policeman on guard duty. How did you get past him?'

'Police?' Clive's voice was just a half-tone below the pitch where it would shatter glass. 'What are the police doing here?'

'We didn't see any police,' Whit growled. 'Why *are* they here?'

'There's been a death—' I wished I'd never mentioned the police, but they were going to find out for themselves, now that they were inside the house.

'A death?' Clive's voice peaked and cracked. 'Is—is Job all right?'

'Job is indestructible,' I reminded him.

'Too bad the same can't be said for the people around him.' Whit did some reminding of his own. It sounded as though Job's jinx had followed him over here, after all.

'Job wasn't anywhere around when it happened,' I said. But was he? He had said that he wasn't far away when he was making that telephone call and that he would be right over. Yet there had been an appreciable length of time before he had shown up. He had told me then that he had been calling from his office but, with all the cellphones about, he could have been much nearer. Near enough to have fired that arrow through the window, then retreated to make another telephone call as an alibi? The shock and dismay he had evinced on learning what had happened had seemed genuine—as well they might if he had just discovered that he had killed the wrong woman. As he had remarked at the Harpo, his eyes weren't what they used to be. And now he had seemingly disappeared from the house.

The kitchen seemed a haven of warmth and comfort. Clive and Whit fell into chairs at the table, looking wet, miserable and wary.

'Gwenda, get a bigger bowl, please, dear.' I concentrated on the immediate practicalities. 'And there are a couple of tins of tuna fish in the cupboard, bring them out and we'll mix them with the eggs—'

'There's cheese in here—' Nova had gone exploring and was rootling through the fridge. 'We can grate it and mix it in, too. And here's half a jar of olives stuffed with pimentoes—'

'Fine.' I took it and popped a couple of olives into my mouth to keep me going. 'We'll chop them and add them. It should be delicious.' And even if it wasn't, I didn't much care. As long as the mayonnaise held out, we were in business.

Gwenda opened the tins, Lucy began slicing bread, Nova chopped olives, I put the kettle on. I noticed that those of us who were busy were keeping calmer than the others. Of course, it must be rather harrowing for a couple of innocent bystanders to walk into a mess like this.

'Where did you say the kids were?' Nova looked pensive. 'I've been thinking. We should take care of them—for Cressie's sake. We ought to take them home with us.'

'Mmm-hmm . . .' I wasn't even going to argue that one. I was going to leave it to Hugh and Martha. 'Why don't you take these sandwiches down the hall to them and suggest it?'

'All right.' She looked at me with sudden suspicion as she took the tray. Was it something I said? Or was it just my tone?

'Come on, Lu.' At least she realized she might need reinforcements.

'Cressie? Did she say Cressie?' Clive and Whit both looked at me in alarm. 'What did she mean by that?'

'Cwumbs! Don't you know?' Gwenda was always ready to leap into a dramatic scene. 'Cwessida is dead! Shot thwough the heart with a bow and awwow!'

'No!' Clive slumped back in his chair as though he had been shot himself. Whit remained upright, but his head began to shake in denial. 'It can't be!'

'I'm afraid it's true.' I concentrated on turning out more sandwiches. It was better than looking at their ashen faces.

'I found them!' Des burst into the kitchen with Job, Griselda and Sergeant Singer behind him. 'They were up at the top of the house—in our flat!'

'We wanted to get away from the hurly-burly,' Job said. 'It was getting so we couldn't hear ourselves think. Hey!' He spotted Clive and Whit. 'Look who's here!' He looked around. 'Where are the others?'

'Roger and Posy went home,' Clive said.

'Roger said he'd ring you tomorrow,' Whit reported.

'Posy said she's going to see you at the auditions Monday and anything you've got in mind can wait until then.'

'Posy is very independent,' Clive said wistfully.

Posy could afford to be; she was doing well. So was Roger. They didn't have to fight their way through the storm to dance attendance on a megalomaniac on the offchance of getting a job.

My sympathy went out to Clive and Whit—until I remembered that Evangeline and I had promised ourselves to Job's new film and I had better save some of that sympathy for myself.

'Food!' Job pounced on a sandwich joyfully, pausing only for a token nod to his hypochondria before stuffing it into his mouth. 'I hope this is low-calorie mayonnaise. You know I gotta watch my cholesterol levels.'

'*You* need not worry about calories or cholesterol.' Griselda pressed a sandwich into Julian Singer's hand. 'You must keep up your strength.'

'Er, thanks . . .' Sergeant Singer took it warily, perhaps wondering why she was so concerned about his strength. I sent a bit of sympathy his way, too. May he never find out.

'Help yourself, Des, Gwenda.' If they didn't get in there fast, there wouldn't be anything left. Even Whit, despite having declared his lack of hunger, seemed to have acquired a sandwich and was gnawing at it. I took one myself and retreated to lean against the wall, near the door, where I could hear anything interesting—like the front door being slammed.

It wasn't long in coming. Nova, with her usual lack of tact, must have broached the subject as she set down the tray.

'Cwumbs! What's that?' Gwenda jumped. In the silence of the kitchen, we could hear the tones of the voices, if not the actual words, as Martha's shrill of indignation, Hugh's snarl of fury, Nova's yelps of protest and Lucy's wail were abruptly cut off by the slam of the front door.

'Nova and Lucy just left,' I said.

'Are they allowed to?' Des asked uncertainly.

'Hmm? Oh—' Belatedly, Sergeant Singer noticed that the question had been addressed to him. 'Oh yes. We finished with them a long time ago. I hadn't realized they were still hanging around until I came in here. There was no reason for them to. We shan't want to see them again.'

'And so say all of us,' I agreed. The faintest comforting murmurs reached me as Hugh and Martha returned to the children, closing that door softly behind them.

'Any more tea?' Job was only interested in his own problems. 'I hope it's decaffeinated. The old system isn't what it used to be. I can't take the rough stuff any more.'

'Don't be silly, Job, you'll outlive us all.'

'Possibly.' He gave me an assessing stare and I was torn between indignation and the thought that, if I could manage to look sufficiently frail, he might be afraid to risk putting me in that new picture.

'Naw, Trixie—' he dashed my hopes. 'You got the right genes. You'll go on for ever too. But, you gotta admit, we've seen a few of the younger ones off in our time.'

'That's a *wotten* thing to say! With poor Cwessida not even cold yet!'

'Very bad taste,' Des said. 'I think you ought to apologize.'

'Who to?' Job was amazed. 'And why? What's it to you?'

'You've offended the ladies.' Des flushed, but held his ground.

'Are you offended?' Job turned to me.

'Yes,' I said, 'I believe I am.'

'Und so am I,' Griselda said.

'It was a wotten thing to say!'

'OK, OK, I apologize. How was I to know you were all such sensitive flowers? I wasn't even thinking about poor Cressida, you know.'

Clive and Whit hadn't said anything, but they were looking quite peculiar. Perhaps they had been offended, too, but had not felt that they were in a position to register a protest.

'So, OK.' Job decided to forgive us all. 'They've got spunk—' He nodded affably at Gwenda and Des. 'I like that in a youngster.'

Clive sat up straighter, angling his head to display his favoured profile. Whit wriggled his shoulders and put on a cocky grin. They were obviously trying to project youth and spunk. From the distance of, say, the Upper Gallery, it might have worked. In close-up . . . Well, it's a tough profession, and if you let things like that get to you, you'd spend most of your time in tears.

'How are the sandwiches holding out?' I asked briskly. 'Shall I make some more?'

'*They* may not require anything more to eat—' Evangeline spoke from the doorway. 'However, I have had nothing yet. I hope there is something left for me?'

'Coming right up.' When I saw the others doing their imitations of the locust swarms in *The Good Earth*, I had hidden a couple of sandwiches away for just such a contingency.

Detective-Superintendent Heyhoe was standing behind Evangeline but, after one look at his face, I decided against offering him anything to eat. He did not seem too pleased to discover Sergeant Singer stuffing his face.

'Sergeant,' he said, with dangerous calm. 'Sergeant, we can't seem to find your Statements.'

'Statements?' Sergeant Singer echoed blankly.

CHAPTER 18

'Statements,' Superintendent Heyhoe confirmed grimly. 'You remember those things they taught you about when you started in the Force? The Statements you take from Witnesses—as soon as possible?' He looked from Sergeant Singer's face to mine—which was equally blank. 'You were first on the scene. You *did* take Statements from Miss Sinclair and Miss Dolan?'

'Y-yes, sir. Er, n-no, sir. Um, that is—'

'It all happened so fast.' I tried to rescue him. 'Sergeant Singer got here just a minute or two before you arrived. He didn't have time to take any statements. And then everything got so confused—'

'No Statements,' Heyhoe said bleakly. 'That explains why we couldn't find them, doesn't it? Singer, I want a word with you.' He turned on his heel and marched away. Sergeant Singer followed, looking miserable.

'Cwumbs!' Gwenda said. 'He's going to tear another stwip off him! Poor old Singer—there won't be anything left of him but shweds. The Superintendent is fuwious!'

'He's always furious.' Evangeline munched her sandwich complacently. 'He's the worst-tempered policeman I ever met. I wonder if he has an ulcer?'

'I'd bet on it.' If he hadn't had an ulcer before he met Evangeline, it was a dead cert she'd given him one. Sergeant Singer was doing his share to help, too.

'I don't like to complain,' Job said. 'But can't we move somewhere a little more comfortable? This chair is breaking my butt.'

'We shall all adjourn to the living-room.' Evangeline rose majestically and led the way.

'But won't Superintendent Heyhoe object?' I tried to stop them. 'Are the police finished in there?'

'If Hoo-ey objects, we'll learn about it soon enough. But I don't see why he should. Everyone has gone, leaving the room in a disgusting condition—just like men—for someone else to clean up.'

'The body—' Griselda held back from a doorway, for perhaps the first time in her life. 'Has the body been removed?'

'Ages ago,' Evangeline assured her blithely. Too blithely. She was first into the room and chose a chair from which she did not have to look at the fatal door. The rest of us weren't so lucky.

'Oh! That's *wevolting!*' Gwenda stared hypnotized at the outline of Cressida's body chalked on the door. A small circle marked the gouge where the arrow had penetrated deep into the wood, brownish-red stains streaking down from it.

'I told you they left the place a mess.' With her back to the offending sight, Evangeline was the most self-possessed person in the room.

'Mein Gott!' Griselda was pale. 'Do something! Cover it!'

'Poor kid, poor kid.' Job shook his head sorrowfully, but his sidelong glance at Griselda was speculative.

'How horrible!' Clive gasped. 'Horror—'

Whit collapsed into a chair as though his knees had suddenly buckled under him. His face was as white as Clive's.

'I'll get something to cover it with,' Des said, then looked uncertain. 'But—?'

'Get the bedspread from my room,' I directed. 'We can tack it up until the police tell us we can wash the door . . . or paint it . . . or replace it . . .'

'Or move house.' Evangeline obviously had been giving the matter some consideration.

'A self-contained flat.' I had to agree with her. 'In a proper apartment building.' There were too many memories accumulating around this place—none of them pleasant.

'Oh no, Twixie,' Gwenda wailed. 'Oh, I don't blame you. I wish I could afford to move, too. But we'll miss you so . . .'

'And we'll miss you,' Evangeline said unconvincingly. 'Nevertheless, I am afraid one cannot escape the conclusion that this house is jinxed.' She glanced at Job as she voiced the word so often associated with him.

'It wouldn't surprise me if you're right.' He did not appear to take it personally. 'I've had some experiences with jinxes in my time and, believe me, once a jinx wraps itself around a place—or a person—it's a damned hard thing to get rid of.'

'Precisely.' Evangeline was now watching him openly, waiting for him to give himself away.

I was far more concerned about Clive and Whit, who were showing signs of impending nausea. The blood had drained from their faces and gave no indication of returning. Tiny beads of sweat rimmed their hairlines. They were swallowing, great dry swallows. Although they tried not to look, they kept darting glances at the door and its grim outline. I hoped they weren't going to be sick on the carpet.

I ought to be used to it by this time, but it never ceases to amaze me, the way actors who play bold, daring heroes, swarming up ropes with sword and cutlass, can go to pieces at the sight of real blood.

'Here we are.' Des returned with my bedspread, a pale blue satin frivolity, incongruous for the use that was to be made of it. 'I found some drawing pins, too.' He walked over to the door and, with a shudder, raised the end of the bedspread to a corner of the door frame. 'I'll just—'

'STOP!' Superintendent Heyhoe thundered from the other doorway. 'Don't touch that door! Trying to tamper with the evidence, are you?'

'No, honestly—' Des dropped the bedspread in his alarm, it billowed cloudlike around his feet. 'I was just going to cover this—this—' He broke off; he didn't know what to call it.

'What are you doing in here anyway?' Heyhoe charged into the room, glaring at all of us impartially. Sergeant Singer slunk in behind him, the picture of a whipped cur. 'You're not supposed to be in here!'

'Sorry—' Clive and Whit surged to their feet. It was their mistake.

'Who are you?' They drew Heyhoe's wrath. 'What are you doing here?'

'Job wanted to see us,' Clive said.

'I wanted to see you hours ago,' Job grumbled. 'You took your time getting here.'

'We got a message—at the theatre,' Whit said.

'You shoulda got the one I left at the pub a lot earlier.'

'We didn't—'

'What pub?' They both spoke at once, too quickly, too defensively.

'Job wanted to talk to you,' I said thoughtfully. 'And he told you Cressida was here—and *you* wanted to talk to *her*.'

'Who *are* these people?' Heyhoe demanded.

'Clive Anderson and Whitby Grant, sir.' Sergeant Singer supplied the identification eagerly. 'They're actors—'

Heyhoe sighed deeply.

'You remember, sir, that television series, *The Highwayman*. They starred in it with the deceased. And all those films, earlier than that: *Bowmen of England* and—'

'*Bowmen?*' Heyhoe was instantly alert. 'As in bow and arrow?'

'Yes, sir. It was an early postwar production. After *Henry V* did so well in the foreign markets, a smaller studio did *Bowmen of England* as an Eady Quota rip-off, but—'

'That's enough, Singer!'

Clive and Whit had slumped back into their chairs. Superintendent Heyhoe strode over to gloat down on them.

'So you worked with the deceased . . .'

'It was years and years ago.' Clive shrank back.

'We never see her these days.' Whit spoke with difficulty, as though his mouth had gone dry. 'Never.'

'But you wanted to talk to her.' Heyhoe hadn't missed a trick. 'What about?'

'O-old time . . .' Clive was trying to brazen it through. 'The old series . . .'

'He means *The Highwayman*, sir.' Sergeant Singer was working hard to redeem himself. 'There are plans to reissue it. That is . . .' He frowned. 'There were. I heard the plan had run into trouble.'

'What trouble?' Heyhoe snapped.

Everyone in the room could answer that question, but there was an uneasy silence.

'Singer?'

'I'm trying to remember, sir. It seems there was a lot of money involved. Residuals, you know.'

'OK, OK. Cressida was blocking the re-release,' Job explained. 'She had the right to, it was in her contract. But that was nothing, she would come round.' But Job's voice held sudden doubt.

'Of course she would have—if we could have got through to her,' Clive said. 'But she wouldn't take telephone calls from us. We sent registered letters, but she never answered. We—'

'Shut up!' Whitby Grant began to crack. 'We should never have come here. I told you that. I didn't want to.'

'Which time?' I asked coldly. My sympathy for them had begun to evaporate as I remembered the crash of broken glass, the arrow humming past me, and Cressida . . . Cressida . . .

'You got the first message, didn't you?' I asked

relentlessly. 'You came straight over to talk to Job and Cressida both. You thought you could kill two birds with one stone—' I stopped aghast. How clichés can spring to terrible life.

'We didn't mean to!' Clive moaned.

'*You* did it!' Whit abandoned his friend. 'I just came along. We decided to reconnoitre and spy out the lie of the land before we rang the bell. We . . . we stumbled over the bow and . . . and he wondered if he could still use one . . .'

'It was an accident!' Clive insisted.

'But it solved a lot of problems. The reissue of *The Highwayman* can go ahead now.' Whether they would benefit from it was another matter and one I couldn't guess at. There would probably be a platoon of lawyers sorting it out for years.

'It was an accident,' Clive babbled. 'An accident! We . . . we were just fooling around with the bow and arrow—'

It took me a moment to recognize the tune Evangeline was humming under her breath. It was that old 'thirties ditty: *I Didn't Know the Gun Was Loaded (And I'll Never Ever Do It Again)*. She had a point. It was very hard not to notice that an arrow had been fitted into the bowstring.

'We took turns aiming it in at one of the lamps,' Clive was still babbling. 'One of the lamps, I swear it! We . . . we only talked about giving her a fright. We never meant to really shoot at all. My . . . my hand slipped . . . and the arrow was released. It was an accident!'

'I must ask you to come with me,' Superintendent Heyhoe said. 'Both of you. And I must warn you that anything you say . . .' He went into his well-practised routine.

'I told you no one could ever want to murder *me*,' Griselda said smugly.

*

It was nearly dawn by the time the last of them had cleared out. Hugh had taken the children home and, after some discussion, Martha had gone with them.

Evangeline had retreated to her room, while I waited with Job and Griselda until their minicab came to collect them. After they had gone, the house seemed empty and echoing. I enjoyed it for a minute, then went to find Evangeline. Once again, I had tidings to impart.

'You still up, Trixie?' She should talk, she was sitting up in bed, reading.

'Not for much longer,' I assured her. 'Would you like a cup of tea before I turn in?'

'Don't be ridiculous.' She reached for a glass of brandy on her bedside table.

'It was just a thought.' I helped myself to a splash of brandy, too, just to be sociable—and to brace myself.

'I was talking to Job about the film,' I said.

'Yes? She waited for it.

'I finally got an idea of the story. He says the vampire theme is the hottest thing going, so it's based on that. Also, *Dracula* is in the public domain. Guess what? Griselda is going to play Dracula's mother!'

'Hah! Typecasting!' Evangeline chortled.

'And we're his aunts.' That wiped the smirk off her face.

'I believe I'm getting a headache.'

'Well, it's better than *Queen Leah!*' Anything would be.

'I'm not so sure.'

'Maybe you'd like to get hold of Lucy and Nova. They could rewrite it as *Draculetta.*'

'*Draculetta!*' We were overtired and we'd both had too much to drink and not enough to eat. Suddenly, we were swept by fits of giggles, like hysterical schoolgirls. I was glad that Martha wasn't around to disapprove.

'Ah, well,' Evangeline said, wiping her eyes. 'We really

must have a serious discussion with Hugh. It's time we got on with *Arsenic and Old Lace*.'

'Maybe, instead of house-hunting, we ought to go theatre-hunting for him.' I was in full agreement with her.

The sooner we got that show on the road, the better.